# "This is very important to me."

Taylor opened her mouth to tell Nick no. But his closeness drove the words from her lips. "I don't—"

"Now is not the time to decide this. I'll pick you up at six and we'll have dinner. What would dinner hurt? Give me a chance to change your mind. That's not too much to ask, is it?"

She must have nodded, because he smiled that killer smile. Taylor wondered if she'd just lost her mind.

The proposal didn't make any sense. But then neither did her reaction. When his gaze had locked on hers and he stood so close, for one brief moment she'd been seriously tempted to throw caution to the wind and say yes.

**Books by Cynthia Rutledge**

Love Inspired

*Unforgettable Faith* #102
*Undercover Angel* #123
*The Marrying Kind* #135

## CYNTHIA RUTLEDGE

lives in the Midwest and has enjoyed reading romance since her teens. She loves the fact that you can always count on a happy ending.

Writing inspirational romance has been especially gratifying because it allows her to combine her faith in God with her love of romance.

# The Marrying Kind
## Cynthia Rutledge

Love Inspired®

Published by Steeple Hill Books™

STEEPLE HILL BOOKS

Steeple
Hill™

ISBN 0-373-87142-2

THE MARRYING KIND

**Printed in U.S.A.**

To my husband, Kirt, for his love and support

# Chapter One

*Could her life get any worse?*

Kaye "Taylor" Rollins outlined her lips in the ornate mirror gracing one wall of the executive washroom, amazed her trembling hand could still draw such a precise cinnamon line. Her hands shook as badly as an alcoholic in the throes of withdrawal, and ripples of panic were rapidly turning her skin to gooseflesh.

She tried to rein in her mounting fear. Surely, the man would listen to reason. To toss her out with no more thought than last night's garbage made no sense.

Her stomach flip-flopped, and Taylor lurched over the sink, fighting to keep down her breakfast. After several deep breaths the bile in the back of her throat retreated, leaving only the fear.

*Dear God, what am I going to do?*

The answer rose from deep within her. *God hath not given us the spirit of fear, but of power, and of love, and of sound mind.*

Taylor's fingers abandoned their death grip on the sink and suddenly she felt incredibly foolish. Why was it so easy for her to forget she wasn't in this alone? Even though she firmly believed the Lord helped those who helped themselves, she never would have made it through this last year without Him at her side. Today would be no different. He would be there with her when she walked into that large office on the twelfth floor.

Taylor straightened and wiped her mouth with a tissue, taking off most of the lipstick she'd so painstakingly applied. Even though she'd never met the company's young CEO, the man had a reputation for fairness. She had nothing to fear from Nicholas Lanagan III. And right now he was the one person with the power to make this wrong right.

Taylor scooped up the pink slip and headed out the door of the washroom to the elevator. Pushing the button with unnecessary vigor, Taylor stared at the piece of paper in her hand—''Effective immediately, your position has been eliminated....''

She crumpled the slip and lifted her chin. With the Lord on her side and Rollins blood coursing through her veins, this latest adversity was not the end of her world. It was just one more obstacle to overcome.

Nicholas Lanagan shifted impatiently and waited for the brass elevator doors to open. He glanced at his watch and scowled. It made good business sense to belong to the Chamber, but when these breakfast meetings ran an hour over and threw his tight schedule into disarray he had to wonder if doing his civic duty was worth it. He'd now play catch-up the rest of the day.

The doors parted smoothly, and Nick exited the elevator with long purposeful strides. He stopped in front of his secretary's large cherry-wood desk. "Good morning, Miss Dietrich."

The older woman calmly pushed the hold button on her phone and raised her steely-eyed gaze. The picture of a woman in control, Miss Dietrich's lined face showed no expression. She didn't waste her time, or his, returning the greeting.

"Mr. Lanagan, Mr. Waters is holding on your line. He says it's important." The woman's finger-nail poised above the transfer button. "Do you want to take the call?"

Nick fought back a surge of irritation. Henry Waters had been a thorn in his side for months, and Nick was at the end of his rope. But the bottom line was he needed Henry's company to solidify Lanagan Associates's place in the increasingly competitive enterprise software market. To risk alienating the man would be reckless. Impulsive. It would be tantamount to business suicide.

"Put him through."

The door swung shut and Nick settled into his soft leather desk chair and took a deep breath. "Henry, what's up?"

The voice on the line radiated excitement. "I know we're meeting this afternoon, but I've got good news and it just couldn't wait."

Nick's grip relaxed around the receiver. "What is it?"

"Claire's coming home!" The restraint Henry normally used in his dealings with Nick had vanished. "I've been waiting for her to come to her senses. When she broke up with you and left town—"

"Henry." Nick spoke more sharply than he'd intended. "That was a long time ago."

The man didn't seem to notice his abruptness.

"Barely six months. There's no reason you can't pick up where you left off."

The cold chill that shot up Nick's spine had nothing to do with the room's temperature. This could be a major complication. But the ability to respond under pressure had always been Nick's strength. He ad-libbed, loosely covering the receiver with one hand and talking to the picture of his father on his desk as if the man had suddenly sprung to life.

"Can't it wait? I'm on the phone." Nick forced an irritated sigh. "Henry, I'm sorry to cut this short, but something's come up. We're still meeting at three?"

"I'll be there," Henry said, disappointment evident in his tone. "We can have a long talk then."

Henry's announcement was still ringing in Nick's ears when Miss Dietrich came in with a steaming cup of coffee. Two sugars already added, just as he liked it.

"It's very hot." She handed him the mug.

"Good." Nick ignored her warning and recklessly took a gulp, almost relishing the scalding sensation searing his throat; the pain took his mind off the implications of Henry's news.

"Anything else, sir?"

"Not now. I'll buzz if I need you."

Miss Dietrich nodded and pulled the door shut behind her. If only he could get rid of Claire with so little effort. Say a few select words and she'd be history. Out of his life for good this time. If only it could be that easy.

He plopped the cup down. The freshly ground Colombian coffee sloshed over the rim and spilled onto the hand-rubbed cherry-wood desktop.

He stifled a curse.

*Claire!* One word said it all. Raking back a strand of hair that dared fall across his forehead, he railed against the injustice. What had he done to deserve this?

Even as he asked, he knew the answer. He'd made the mistake of escorting the attractive brunette to a few social functions. All of a sudden they'd been labeled a couple. Dating the daughter of a potential business partner was risky under the best of circumstances, but when that woman was Henry Waters's little princess the potential for disaster increased tenfold.

When Claire had unexpectedly accepted a job at a prestigious public relations firm in Washington, D.C., no one had been more thrilled than he'd been.

An added plus was that Henry had been incredibly sympathetic when his daughter had taken off without a second thought. In retrospect, Nick couldn't help but wonder if that had given him an advantage in the bidding war for Henry's company.

Taking over Waters Inc.'s data warehousing niche in the enterprise software business had long been Nick's dream. Now, after endless negotiations and countless months of contract revisions, he stood on the verge of translating that dream into reality. The merger would be finalized in less than two months.

*Unless Henry backed out.*

Nick blew out a harsh breath. If the man took his business elsewhere, Lanagan Associates would be forced into major restructuring. Today's layoffs would be nothing compared to the massive cuts he'd be forced to make.

Why did she have to come back now? Like a dark storm cloud, thoughts of Claire Waters swirled in his head.

She could ruin it all.

*If he let her.*

Nick quenched his rising annoyance. He could stop her. She'd fare no better than any of the others who'd tried to come between him and what he wanted.

He'd come up with a solution.

He always did.

The office door flew open and slammed shut. Erik Nordstrom, his closest friend and chief legal counsel, splayed himself against it, looking more like a spy on the run than a corporate attorney in an Armani suit. "Quick, bolt the door. Your watchdog is ready to bite."

"Watchdog?"

"That drill sergeant you call a secretary." Erik heaved a theatrical sigh and pretended to wipe some sweat from his brow. "I wasn't on your appointment calendar. It's a crime, you know. Opening the door to your office if you're not on her schedule."

"She's just doing her job." Nick sighed and gestured to a nearby chair. "Since you're here, you might as well sit down. My morning's shot, anyway."

"I'm glad to see you, too." Erik slanted a glance at Nick and claimed his favorite leather wing chair. Up went his Italian loafers on a glass table. "What's got you so bummed?"

"Claire Waters. She's coming back."

"So?"

"So—" Nick tried to hide his irritation "—Henry thinks we should pick up where we left off."

Erik's hazel eyes flickered behind his thin wire-rimmed glasses. "But it's been months since the Catwoman left."

Nick's lips twitched at Erik's not so fond nick-name for Claire. His friend had taken an instant dislike to the woman.

"If I remember right, you weren't sorry to see her go," Erik added.

"I know that. You know that. The only one who doesn't know that is Henry. And maybe Claire." Nick rubbed his neck. "Henry's thinking Claire and I are going to have some glorious reunion and live happily ever after."

Erik stifled a laugh. "He obviously doesn't know you're already committed."

"Committed? What are you talking about?" Nick frowned. "I'm not engaged."

"All right. Maybe the company is more like a mistress. It gets all your attention, your devotion." Erik placed one hand on his chest and topped it with the other. "Just tell Claire there's no room in your heart for anyone else."

"Cut it out, Erik. This is serious. There's no way I'm going to let Claire's return ruin everything."

"Maybe she doesn't want you, either. Have you thought about that?"

Nick shook his head, wishing that were true. "I didn't get that impression."

"Okay, then…" Erik paused for a moment. "What's the worst that could happen? She comes. She hits on you. You turn her down."

"And the merger negotiations fall apart." Nick pressed his fingertips to his temples. "You know what Henry's like. He'll take any rejection of his daughter as a personal slight."

"Okay, then string her along. Whisper a few sweet nothings in her ear. Just enough to keep her happy until those papers are signed."

"It's tempting." Nick knew it would be the easiest solution, one with the least amount of risk. Still, something held him back. "But I couldn't do that, even to Claire. Besides, I might get stuck with her forever."

Erick visibly shuddered. "A life with that woman would be a fate worse than death."

"I agree wholeheartedly." Nick laughed. "Just don't let Henry know I said so."

"So, what are you going to do?" Erik glanced

curiously Nick's way. "If I know you, you've already got a plan."

"Something did occur to me when you were talking about being married to the company."

"I was just kidding about using that excuse."

"Still, it did give me an idea." Nick leaned forward and rested his elbows on the desk. He lowered his voice, even though they were the only ones in the room. "I could tell Henry I'm engaged."

"Won't work." Erik shook his head. "He'll insist on meeting her."

"I'll say she doesn't live here."

"Henry might buy it, but Claire? Not on your life."

Nick thought for a moment. "Then I'll find someone in Cedar Ridge to play the part."

His friend collapsed against the smooth leather, his mouth twisting in a wry grin. "It has potential. The only problem is you haven't even been seeing anyone lately."

"Henry doesn't know that."

"Fiancée's usually expect marriage as a follow-up."

"This one won't. I'll make that very clear."

"So—do you have anyone at all in mind?"

Nick shook his head. "I haven't gotten that far."

"How about that redhead you brought to the Christmas party?"

"Aimee?" Nick shook his head. "I don't think so."

"Why not?" Erik quirked an eyebrow, and a mischievous grin danced on his lips. "She was really hot."

"Keep in mind the reason we broke up."

"Because you were more interested in work than her."

The promptness of his friend's response brought back Nick's smile. "Not that reason."

"All right, so she was more interested in your money than you." Erik's eyes gleamed. "In this situation, she'd be perfect."

"Probably. But she's out, anyway. I heard she's getting married next month. For real."

"You really think you'll be able to come up with a fiancée on such short notice?"

Nick met Erik's questioning gaze with determination. "I don't have much choice. I'll find someone if I have to take the next female that walks through that door."

Their gaze shifted to the door and—as if on cue—it opened.

"Mr. Lanagan, I'm so sorry. I told her you were in conference." Miss Dietrich cast a disapproving glance at the young woman standing unannounced in the doorway's arch.

Obviously pretty.

Obviously furious.

Chestnut curls, highlighted with rich strands of deep red, tumbled past stiffened shoulders in loose waves. Delicately carved facial bones surrounded large almond-shaped eyes of glittering emerald-green.

The hand-tailored jacket's cut and rich sable color accentuated the woman's slim waist and gently flaring hips. Brushed with a hint of copper, her full lips tightened under his scrutiny.

"Mr. Lanagan, I apologize for interrupting, but I must speak with you." The woman's chin lifted a notch.

"Would you like me to call security, sir?" The look in Miss Dietrich's eyes clearly said he'd be a fool if he didn't.

Nick glanced at Erik, and his lips twitched when he received a subtle thumbs-up. His gaze settled on the intruder, and her eyes darkened to a frosty jade.

"No, Miss Dietrich. I think I want to hear what Miss—"

"Rollins." She paused.

Nick shot a quick glance at Erik. Was the name supposed to mean something to him? His friend shrugged.

Nick checked his watch. "I have a few minutes I can spare. Miss Dietrich, hold my calls."

"Very well, sir." His secretary shot Taylor a narrowed glance. "I'll be right outside if you need me."

''Ms. Rollins, have a seat.'' Nick gestured to the chair in front of his desk.

The woman stepped forward, a belligerent look in her eye, and sat down. Undisguised interest glimmered behind Erik's gold spectacles.

Nick jerked his head toward the doorway. ''Erik. We'll continue our discussion later.''

Apparently not the least bit disturbed over his abrupt dismissal, Erik stood and walked toward the door, flashing Nick a knowing grin. He grasped the doorknob and turned, tipping his head toward the woman. ''Ms. Rollins, a pleasure. And, Nick, good luck.''

Nick ignored the comment and directed his attention to his visitor. ''Normally I don't meet with anyone without an appointment.''

A small muscle jumped at the corner of her jaw, but her voice was soft and controlled. ''I realize that, however this is very important.''

He smiled, hoping to put her at ease. ''You have my undivided attention. What can I do for you?''

A pink slip sailed across his slick desktop. ''You can explain what this is all about.''

Nick reached out and picked up the computer-generated form. He suppressed a groan. This was just the reason he'd instructed Personnel not to deliver the termination notices until the end of the day.

He laid the slip on the desk and studied her. "Oh, so that's it."

"Yes. That's it."

He adjusted his cuffs and straightened the knot on his tie. "Well, Kay—"

Irritation flickered across her expression, then disappeared. "I prefer to be called Taylor. Assuming, of course, that you want to be on a first name basis, *Nick.*"

"This form says *Kay.*" He glanced at the sheet.

"Kaye is my given name. But I've always gone by Taylor." The slight tightening in her jaw indicated she probably wasn't as calm and serene as she appeared. "And another thing, if you're firing someone, I'd suggest spelling their name correctly. My first name is *K-A-Y-E,* not *K-A-Y.*"

"Well, *Taylor.*" Nick reclined slightly in his chair. "We have a volatile marketplace out there. I'm sure you're aware that certain measures must be taken for a company to be competitive."

Her emerald eyes raked him. "Don't patronize me, *Nick.* I'm not a naive little girl. I know what the marketplace is like. That's why I checked this job out carefully before I even considered it."

"If you'll—"

"I'm not finished. I gave up a good position to move back to Cedar Ridge. For what? For you to fire me after only three weeks? What's fair about that? I have bills to pay. Lots of bills." Her voice broke slightly then steadied. "I never would have taken this job if I'd known a cutback was in the works."

*Bills.* Any sympathy he'd started to muster vanished and he regarded her through narrowed eyes.

"You had to know this position was going to be eliminated. Why did you even fill it?" Her voice cracked, and she pressed her lips together.

"We hired you only three weeks ago?"

She nodded.

"I apologize for the mix-up." He made a mental note to check with Personnel. They were only supposed to have been filling key positions, not ones scheduled for elimination. "Unfortunately I don't have another job for you. After this downsizing is completed, we'll be in a hiring freeze until the end of the summer."

Her face paled, and she took a ragged breath. Despite the fact he had no tolerance for those who lived beyond their means, Nick found himself feeling almost sorry for her. For all he knew, she could be the sole support of a couple of kids. "Unless..."

"I'm willing to consider almost anything. I'm very versatile." Desperation made her voice husky.

He studied her intently for a moment, then slowly shook his head. "No, on second thought, I don't think it would be a good idea."

"Listen, I *really* need the money. I told you, I'll

consider almost anything." Emotion whipped color into her cheeks in an appealing dusty-pink glow.

Nick leaned back and wondered if he'd taken leave of his senses. He was crazy to even think it might work.

"At least let me interview. Give me that chance." Her words stopped just short of begging, and her stricken eyes told him what it had cost her.

Nick tapped his pen on the desk, then without further thought plunged recklessly ahead. "Let's start with you telling me a little bit about yourself. That'll help me determine if you'd be right for this, ah, assignment."

She took a deep breath and flashed him a grateful smile. He found himself smiling back.

"I graduated from Swarthmore with a degree in computer engineering. I worked for ComTECH Industries in Denver for the past three years."

Nick raised one eyebrow. "I don't understand. With those credentials, I wouldn't think you'd have any problem finding suitable employment."

"Probably not," she agreed. "If I moved back to Denver. But right now I can't do that."

"I take it, then, your husband isn't willing to move?" He could almost hear his personnel director scream at the question.

"I'm not married."

He leaned back in his chair. "So, what's the problem?"

"I'm an only child. My mother died when I was fifteen. Last year, my father was killed in a car accident." She clasped her hands together and took a deep breath. "My grandparents are getting older, and I'm their only relative now. I want—I need—to be close to them."

Nick's eyes narrowed speculatively, "What about evenings? Would you be free at night if the job demanded it? Or do you have to help care for them?"

She laughed, a full-throated laugh that brought a smile to his lips. "Heavens, no. They're not dependent on me at all. But after my father's death, my grandfather suffered a mild heart attack. He recovered fully, but it was hard being two hours away."

Nick stared thoughtfully. His gaze traveled over her face and searched her eyes. *It just might work.* "Well, Taylor, I think I may have a job for you."

Her face lit up, and a soft gasp escaped her. "You mean, you've already decided? The job is mine?"

"It is. That's of course assuming you want it." Would she agree? Was she really that desperate? His pulse quickened.

Her whole face spread into a smile. "Want it? Of course I do. Tell me about it. What position would I fill?"

"The position is—" his gaze met her questioning eyes "—my fiancée."

# Chapter Two

"What did you say?"

Nick repeated the words slowly, as if that would increase her comprehension. "I'm offering you a job. You'd be my fiancée. Just for the summer."

Taylor's heart quickened, and for the briefest of moments she allowed herself to wonder what it would be like to be this man's fiancée. With his classically handsome features, jet-black hair and piercing blue eyes, Nick Lanagan epitomized every woman's dream man.

"Shall we talk salary then?" A satisfied smile creased his lips, and he picked up his pen as if he planned to write out a check.

"No," she blurted, her voice stiff and unnatural even to her own ears. She realized her hesitation had given him the mistaken impression she was considering his outrageous offer. "Mr. Lanagan—"

Nick leaned back in his chair and chuckled. "First names, Taylor. No one will believe we're engaged if you're calling me Mr. Lanagan."

Irritation surged at the cool confidence reflected in his smile. "*Mr. Lanagan,* if this is some kind of sick joke, I'm not laughing."

"Wait a minute." His blue eyes flashed. "You're the one who said you needed money."

"Yes, but I believe I also said I wanted a job."

"That's what I'm offering." His gaze challenged her. "A job for the summer. Nothing more. Nothing less."

"As your paid honey."

"As my fiancée."

"Why me? You must have dozens of girls who'd like to play house with you."

His eyes glinted to steel-gray, and she smiled to herself. Good. She'd gotten under his skin.

"Absolutely. But they might expect more from me than a salary. And a paycheck is all I'm prepared to provide."

"A paycheck to pose as your fiancée?" She studied him thoughtfully like he was one of her data sheets she was having difficulty deciphering. What the man was proposing made absolutely no sense. She knew she should end the conversation now. But her insatiable curiosity wouldn't allow it. "Why would a man in your position need to hire a fiancée? And what kind of services would you expect this fiancée to provide?''

''Provide?''

''Don't give me that innocent look. You know very well what I'm asking. Is sex part of the deal?''

Nick threw back his head and laughed. His lips parted in a dazzling display of straight, white teeth. ''No.'' He rose and leaned across the desk, ''All I'd ask is the pleasure of your company. Maybe a few public kisses. A little hand holding. Nothing more.''

''This is ridiculous. I came here asking for a job. A real job.''

''At least consider my offer.''

Her gaze lingered a moment before she shook her head and rose. ''I know I told you I was desperate. And I am, but even desperate has its limits.''

''Aren't you being a bit hasty? We haven't even discussed how much this arrangement would be worth to me.''

''No amount of money—''

''Twenty thousand dollars a month.''

Her breath caught in her throat, and she grasped the back of the chair for support. That kind of money would make a serious dent in her bills.

A deep, rich fragrance enveloped her, and she looked up. Nick stood beside her, so close she could see the flecks of hazel in his blue eyes. A shiver rippled down her spine.

"This is very important to me," he said in a husky baritone. "Just think about it."

She opened her mouth to tell him that more time wouldn't matter, the answer would still be no. But his closeness drove the words from her lips.

"I don't—"

"I agree. Now is not the time to decide this." His hand rested firmly against her back, and he propelled her toward the door. "I'll pick you up at six and we'll have dinner. I guarantee I'll be able to put all your fears to rest."

Obviously he didn't realize there was nothing to discuss. Her mind was made up.

"What would dinner hurt?"

She could feel herself weakening, and as if sensing her weakness, he pressed on. "We'll just talk. Then, if you still decide it's not for you…"

"It's not," she said with more conviction than she felt.

"Give me a chance to change your mind." He ushered her out of the office. "That's not too much to ask, is it?"

She must have nodded, because he smiled that killer smile. He mentioned something about getting her address from Personnel before the door closed softly behind her. Taylor steadied herself against the doorjamb wondering if she'd just lost her mind.

The proposal didn't make any sense. But then neither did her reaction.

When his gaze had locked on hers and he stood so close she could scarcely catch her breath, for one brief moment, she'd been seriously tempted to throw caution to the wind and say yes.

Nick inhaled the rich aroma of Starbucks's finest blend, the dark brew steaming hot. Unlike many of the younger secretaries, Miss Dietrich considered keeping him well supplied with coffee part of her job. The woman was definitely an anachronism. A woman who insisted on being called Miss Dietrich instead of the more informal Margaret or the more modern Ms. A woman who steadfastly refused to call him by his first name. She was a top-notch secretary. And she made a terrific cup of coffee.

Nick grabbed the half-empty carafe and upended it over his mug. "So, what do you think of Ms. Rollins?"

Erik Nordstrom took off his glasses, his normally boisterous demeanor strangely subdued. He flipped the frames from one hand to the other. "She's pretty. Well-educated. Intelligent. I don't think you'll have any trouble convincing people she's your fiancée."

"But..." Nick's eyes narrowed, and he forced the rising irritation down. If Erik had reservations,

Nick needed to hear them. The trouble was, he'd already made his decision.

Eyeglasses in place, Erik crossed his arms behind his head. "One thing bothers me. She must be desperate for cash to even consider your offer. The question is why?"

Nick snorted. "Probably overextended on her credit cards. That suit she had on certainly didn't come off the rack. My mother was the same way."

Despite Taylor Rollins's reluctance, she'd end up agreeing to his offer. He'd seen the flash of raw hunger when he'd mentioned the twenty thousand dollars.

Erik regarded him with a speculative gaze, and Nick fought to keep his expression impassive. The man knew him all too well. They'd been friends since their freshman year in college.

"The reason doesn't matter, anyway. This is strictly a business proposition." Nick's gaze dared him to disagree.

"You seriously want me to believe you looked at those cat green eyes, those gorgeous legs and those—"

"That's right." Nick snapped.

If Erik heard the harshness in Nick's tone, he ignored it. "Still, you didn't need to ask her to dinner. You could have worked out the details right in your office."

Nick shook his head. "She's a little hesitant.

Dinner will provide the right atmosphere. I'll be charming and the money will do the rest. Remember—as of today—she's out of work.''

"Which brings up another concern." Erik's gaze grew thoughtful. "If she's as desperate for cash as you say, it may have been a huge mistake offering her this, ah, opportunity. Especially since she'd just been fired.''

Nick rubbed his suddenly tense neck. "What do you mean?''

"I'm talking sexual harassment. We may have left ourselves wide open for litigation.''

"Sexual harassment?''

"I know it sounds crazy, but it would be easy for a jury to misconstrue your actions.''

Nick sank into the thick leather of his desk chair and raked his fingers through his hair. Here he'd foolishly believed the day couldn't get any worse. "A lawsuit? That's all I need.''

He cursed his own impulsiveness, knowing he had no one to blame but himself. Nick punched the intercom. "Miss Dietrich, get me Harvey Rust in Personnel.''

Five minutes later, Taylor's file lay open on his desk. Her impressive résumé overflowed with the type of experience and credentials Lanagan Associates sorely needed.

*What doesn't make sense is why we let her go.*

Erik read the application and résumé over his

shoulder. Nick looked up at his friend's sharp intake of air.

"Uh-oh. That's a problem."

Nick frowned and glanced at the records. "What's the matter?"

Erik's finger pointed to the name of Taylor's emergency contact. *William Rollins, grandfather.*

"Who is he?"

"I can't believe you don't recognize the name." Eric's expression reflected his surprise.

"I didn't grow up here, remember? Unlike you, I don't know everybody and his dog."

"But that name should be familiar, even to you. 'Don't mess around with Bill Rollins'?"

A fierce tightness gripped Nick's chest. "The judge that retired last year?"

Erik nodded. "Thirty years on the bench. He's still practicing law, but on a limited basis."

"I remember now. Didn't he have a heart attack or something?"

"That's right. It happened after his son was killed in that big accident on the freeway. His son was Senator Robert Rollins. Don't even try to tell me you don't remember *him*. His death made the wire services from coast to coast." Erik took off his glasses and massaged the bridge of his nose. "This couldn't get much worse."

"You don't think—"

Erik's nod confirmed his fears. "I do think we

may have just delivered Judge Rollins a case he can't resist. And a case he can't lose."

Taylor took a deep breath and straightened her shoulders. Ever since she left the office, her mind had been as tangled and chaotic as her wind-whipped hair.

One moment she was headed home, the top of her convertible down, her favorite radio station blaring full blast. The next, she stood on her grand-parents' steps, her knuckle poised against the six-panel door.

What had propelled her to her Nana and Grandpa Bill's clapboard colonial rather than her own mod-ern town house? She hesitated, tempted to slip away while she still had time, when the door abruptly opened.

Her grandmother, half out the door before she saw Taylor, halted midstep and grabbed the door frame to steady her balance. "Honey, you startled me. I thought you were at work."

"I got off early." Her insides were like a mass of quivering Jell-O, but Taylor was amazed at how calm she sounded. "If you're busy—"

"Nonsense, my dear. I'm delighted to see you."

She wrapped her arm firmly about Taylor's shoulders and gave the younger woman no choice but to be led into the foyer. "I'm just going to run out and get the mail. Your grandpa's expecting an important letter. Lunch will be on the table in a few minutes. Of course, you'll join us?''

Taylor couldn't help but smile. From the time she could walk, Nana had been consistent in her approach to life's problems. It didn't matter what the question or the concern, a little slice of one of her gourmet creations would make it better. It's a wonder they didn't all weigh three hundred pounds! Thankfully, her family seemed to be blessed with a high metabolism. She surveyed her grandmother's trim form out of the corner of her eye. At five feet six inches, Nana never weighed more than one hundred and twenty-five pounds. Despite her silver hair, her trim figure clad in the latest style made her look much younger than her seventy-plus years.

Taylor shifted her gaze to the den. Her grandfather sat hunched over the honey-colored oak desk that had come home with him after his retirement, totally immersed in a thick law book. Like a Norman Rockwell painting, the scene tugged at her heartstrings.

The click-clack of her heels on the hardwood floor must have alerted him. He looked up, and a fond smile lit his still-handsome features. ''Taylor. This is a pleasant surprise. Come and give your grandpa a big hug.''

His strong arms encircled her, and Taylor said a quiet prayer of thanks. Losing her parents had been almost more than she could bear. If she had lost him… She pushed the thought from her mind and hugged his lean frame extra hard.

"You're looking good." She pulled away and held him at arm's length. He reminded her so much of her father. The same nose, the same strong features. Only her father's hair had been dark brown, while Grandpa Bill's chestnut strands were peppered with silver.

"He needs to take it easy if he wants to stay looking that way." Nana said from the doorway, a bundle of letters in one hand.

"Oh, Kaye." Grandpa Bill rolled his eyes.

"You already had one heart attack. I don't want you to have another."

Taylor frowned. "Have you been having more chest pain?"

"No."

"Yes." Nana looked at her husband sternly. "Tell Taylor the truth, Bill."

"Okay, maybe a little now and again. But—" he pulled a small medicine container from his shirt pocket "—the nitro takes care of it right away."

"What does your cardiologist say?" Taylor tried unsuccessfully to keep the anxiety from her voice.

"The doctors say he needs to slow down and not let everything bother him so much." Nana's words were clearly as much for her husband's benefit as for Taylor's.

"Once this case is completed—"

Taylor looked at them questioningly.

"Bill's doing some legal work for a friend. It wasn't supposed to take much time, but—"

"It's almost over, Kaye. Then I'll have time to relax, maybe golf more." He turned to Taylor as if eager to get the focus off himself. "How about you, sweetheart? Been out playing lately?"

"I've been too busy. I think I've only played eighteen a couple times this year."

"I can't imagine what the two of you see in that game." Nana shook her head. "Bill, why don't you and Taylor relax in the living room? I'm going to put the mail away and then I'll make us all some iced tea."

"Sounds good to me," Taylor said.

"My dear." Grandpa Bill crooked his arm, and Taylor took it. They walked to the living room arm in arm. "I remember when we couldn't get you off the links. That new job must be taking up a lot of time. Or perhaps it's not the job. Maybe it's a young man?"

The image of Nick flashed in her mind, and Taylor's face warmed. She forced her attention to her grandfather, noticing the lines of fatigue around his eyes and mouth.

If only man troubles were all she had to worry about. She forced herself to breathe past the sudden tightness in her chest.

"Grandpa Bill—" She stopped, not sure what to say.

"Taylor, is something wrong?" A frown marred his worn face.

Did his complexion suddenly seem more ashen? Her breath caught in her throat. "No, no, everything is going great."

His brows drew together, and his eyes filled with concern. "Princess, you can tell me."

She met his gaze head-on and forced a bright smile. "Everything's just great."

"That's the second time you said that, and I don't believe it for a minute. Something's bothering my girl. I can tell." He pulled her to the couch and made her sit down. His large hand, so like her father's, gently cradled hers. "You just remember, your grandmother and I are always here for you."

She cuddled next to him like she used to when she'd been a little girl. Her head leaned against his shoulder, and his hand lightly stroked her hair. The familiar loving gesture brought tears to her eyes.

"Oh, Grandpa Bill. You're right. It is a man." Her frustrations centered on a man, all right. One man. Nicholas Lanagan III.

A twinkle returned to her grandfather's eyes, and a more reassuring color returned to his face. "I thought as much. Who is he? How long have you been seeing him?"

"Whoa. Hold it a minute, counselor." Taylor

jerked upright and realized he'd completely misunderstood.

"What's going on in here?" Nana strode into the room, a silver tray with a pitcher of tea and three glasses balanced in her hands.

"Taylor's got a new boyfriend. And I've got a hunch it's serious."

A flash of joy erased the worry on Nana's face. She hurried across the room, setting the tray on the credenza, the tea forgotten. "Back up. I want to hear all about him. How you met. How long you've been dating. Don't leave out any details."

Taylor groaned and stalled for time. "What about the iced tea?"

"It can wait." Nana's eyes sparkled.

The love on their faces shone as bright as the afternoon sun, and at that moment Taylor knew she would do anything to spare these two people more hurt. Even if it meant telling a little white lie. Or two. She took a deep breath. "We've been seeing each other casually for some time. It's getting kind of serious."

"Enough of the mystery," Nana said. "Who is he?"

"Do we know him? Does he golf?" Bill added.

Taylor laughed and patted his hand. "You're just looking for someone to round out your foursome."

A brief flash of sorrow skittered across her grandfather's face, and guilt stabbed Taylor. Her father's death had left that slot vacant.

Grandpa Bill seemed to force a smile to his face. "All I want—" he grabbed his wife's hand "—all *we* want is to see you happy. And if this man makes you happy—"

"I think he can, Grandpa Bill. I really think he can." The lies slipped off her tongue so naturally she could almost believe them herself. Taylor paused. She'd nearly passed the point of no return.

Could she do it? Accept an engagement to a man she didn't know? Even for a summer? Her belief in love, commitment and the sanctity of marriage hadn't changed. But love, commitment and the sanctity of marriage didn't enter into this arrangement. After all, she reminded herself, she wouldn't actually be getting married, and even real engagements often were broken. What harm would there be if she agreed to Lanagan's deal? What would happen if she didn't? For a long moment she studied her grandparents, then cast her eyes heavenward.

*Dear God, is this really part of your plan?*

# *Chapter Three*

"**D**rat."

Taylor pulled the linen dress off and tossed it onto her bed with the other discarded outfits in a well-practiced move. If only she'd thought to ask where they were eating this evening.

Her hand reached into the closet, finally settling on a denim dress. With its scoop front bodice, shirred empire waist and long easy skirt, it definitely qualified as casual. The silver leaf buttons dressed it up, and she chose sandals of powder-blue to complete the outfit.

*Hair up or down?* Taylor grabbed a swath and twisted it upward, but released her hold, scattering the curls around her shoulders. Tonight she'd leave it down and pray the humidity left it alone.

She glanced in the mirror and frowned, rubbed

off the pink lipstick and reached for her favorite cinnamon shade.

The doorbell chimed, and Taylor's head shot up. A trail of reddish-brown streaked across her chin. She grabbed a tissue and hurriedly scrubbed her face before heading down the stairs. She stopped in the foyer and cast a quick glance in the mirror. A flush stained her cheeks, and her eyes were brighter than normal.

The way her heart pounded in her chest, you'd think this was a date and not simply a business meeting. She took a deep, steadying breath, pasted a welcoming smile on her face and opened the door.

"Nick. Hello."

Like her, he'd dressed casually. With a blue chambray shirt deepening his eyes to the color of the ocean and his hair gleaming like the surface of her ebony piano, he was even more attractive than in his business suit.

"Come on in."

"I thought we'd start this out right." He held out an assortment of spring flowers interspersed with baby's breath.

"Oh. Thank you." Taylor smiled and took the bouquet. It'd been a long time since a man—other than her grandfather—had surprised her with flowers. She stepped aside to let him pass. "Have a seat and make yourself at home. I'll put these in water."

Taylor gestured to a chair in the living room and

headed for the kitchen. Reaching into the upper cupboard for her mother's crystal vase, she caught a glimpse of him through the colonnade's arch surveying her living quarters. Most of the ornate furniture and limited-edition prints had been her parents'. She'd briefly considered selling them to help pay her father's gambling debts, but immediately discarded the notion. Her grandparents were well aware what these heirlooms meant to her, and no excuse for selling them would have been good enough.

Her hands shook as she quickly arranged the flowers. She adjusted one last sprig of baby's breath and carried the vase into the living room, the keen fresh scent of spring filling the room.

"I grew up with antiques." Nick reverently caressed the smooth finish of an early-nineteenth-century satinwood drum table. "This is beautiful workmanship."

Taylor smiled and set the vase on the mantel. The table had been her mother's favorite. "The inlaid purpleheart wood makes the piece."

"Obviously you like the good stuff. Is that why you need the money?" His arm swept out, encompassing the furnishings. "So you can live like this?"

Taylor took a deep breath and tried to keep the irritation from showing in her face. "I like nice things. And from the looks of your car in my driveway, so do you.''

He didn't tense up. Instead he carefully set down an ornate vase he'd picked up and studied her.

She shifted under his intense gaze. ''The point is it's really none of your business what I need the money for—''

''You're right,'' he said. ''So, you're still considering my offer?''

''Maybe. If you're still willing to pay me twenty thousand dollars a month.''

He hesitated. ''That's what I said.''

''You don't sound so sure anymore.''

''I'm sure. I need a fiancée, and you need money. We're the perfect couple.''

''That's stretching it a little,'' Taylor said dryly, reaching past him for the sweater draped over the back of a chair. ''By the way, I went to see my grandpa this afternoon. I told him about you.''

''You spoke with your grandfather,'' he repeated softly, his eyes flat and expressionless. ''The judge.''

''Do you know him?'' She'd never considered the possibility.

''I've heard of him. We've never met.''

''Well, he wants to meet you. He had a lot of questions—''

''What did you tell him?''

The harshness in his tone took her by surprise. "What could I tell him?"

"Answer my question, Taylor."

His abruptness sent her temper soaring. No wonder the man didn't have a girlfriend. In a few minutes, he wouldn't have a fiancée, temporary or otherwise.

"Wait just one minute, buster. Don't you dare use that tone with me."

His eyes narrowed and his back stiffened ramrod straight. "There was nothing improper about my offer."

Shock tempered her anger. "I'm not saying there was."

"Then what are you saying?"

"We don't know if we even like each other, but you think we can convince our friends and family we're in love? I'm not so sure. I don't know if we can pull this off and I don't want my grandparents hurt."

"Are they suspicious?"

"Not yet." She shook her head, remembering their reaction. "Actually when I told them we were involved, maybe seriously, they were thrilled."

"You told your grandfather we were serious?" The tenseness in his jaw eased, and he expelled a deep breath. "Then his questions—"

Totally bewildered at his reaction, Taylor could only stare. "Were about you. Where you grew up, if you had any brothers or sisters, stuff that I didn't have a clue how to answer.''

''We can take care of that,'' he said with a relieved grin. ''Over dinner I'll bore you with my life story.''

''That's a start, but...'' Taylor paused, refusing to shove aside her concerns. ''What makes you so sure you can convince everyone you're in love with me? You don't even know me.''

''Well.'' A dimple in his cheek flashed. ''I *was* in a few plays back in high school.''

''Oh, I get it,'' she said. ''You'll play Romeo. I'll be Juliet. Is that the plan?''

''I want this to work.'' His eyes blazed with determination. ''And it will.''

Taylor could only shake her head. Nick's confidence and self-assurance reminded her so much of her father. Robert Rollins believed there was no goal too high that it couldn't be reached and no obstacle too large that it couldn't be overcome. Until he'd gotten in way over his head.

Taylor pushed the disturbing thought away and answered Nick's confident smile hesitantly with one of her own. Lying had always been something she abhorred. Still, she needed the money. And who would it hurt? If only she could be as certain as Nick they could pull it off.

They walked in silence to the sleek silver-blue sports car parked at the curb. Taylor waited while he opened the door. She'd barely settled into the plush leather seats of the Jaguar XK8 when an obvious thought struck her and she wondered why she hadn't thought of it before. "I've got an idea. Why don't we treat tonight as a sort of dress rehearsal? We could *act* the part of a couple in love and at the end of the evening critique our performance. Then we'll have a better idea whether or not we can pull this off."

"Sounds good to me." Nick reached over and brought her hand to his mouth, placing a kiss in the palm.

A surge of heat shot up her arm, and Taylor started to pull away, then noticed his impish grin. She chuckled and slipped her hand from his grasp.

Almost reluctantly he flipped the ignition, and the car sped away from the curb.

"Is the Lodge okay?" Nick turned the car off the highway onto a familiar dirt road.

"That's fine."

Built by a handful of wealthy businessmen, the exclusive private club was originally designed as a gathering place for sportsmen. Over the years, the tennis courts and golf course had been added, and the men-only rule had fallen by the wayside. The Lodge housed the Drake restaurant, famous in the region for its wild game cuisine.

He turned slowly onto the spacious grounds, and Taylor lowered the window. The soft fragrance of lilacs teased her nose, and she inhaled deeply. She reveled in the refreshing scent and ignored the breeze mussing her hair.

The headlights illuminated the award-winning golf course that lined both sides of the gently winding drive. She smiled as the eighth hole came and went. She'd had her first and only hole-in-one there. A sixteenth birthday present to herself.

"You look lovely tonight." Nick's voice broke into her thoughts.

Taylor had to give him points for trying. He'd clearly jumped into the role of adoring fiancée while she sat there blushing like some awestruck schoolgirl out for the first time.

She forced herself to envision what she would say—how she would react—if she loved this stranger sitting beside her. Taking a deep breath, she tentatively slid closer and leaned her head against his shoulder. It seemed unnatural to be so physically close to someone she'd just met, but she reminded herself it was no different than sitting in a crowded stadium at a Broncos game shoved up against some stranger.

But no stranger at a game had ever smelled so good or made her heart race so fast. Nick turned his head, and she could sense his gaze, but instead of looking up, she snuggled closer.

With a push of a button, Nick filled the Jag with

strains of Beethoven's *Eroica* symphony, her favorite piece.

She raised her head and smiled. "Oh, you like classical music?"

"Actually I do. But I can switch—"

"No," she said before he could change the CD. "I like it, too. A lot."

His lips curved in a self-satisfied smile before he turned his attention to the road. Taylor returned her head to his shoulder and let the music transport her away from her worries, soothing the tightness in her limbs, allowing her to relax fully for the first time since she'd opened that envelope with the pink slip stuffed inside.

The car rounded the horseshoe shaped drive in front of the Lodge, and Taylor reluctantly straightened. Turning the car over to valet parking, Nick offered his arm to Taylor and they walked into the Great Room of the Lodge.

Nick stepped forward to give the maître d' their names. Taylor scanned the crowded room, hoping she wouldn't see anyone she knew. Breathing a sigh of relief, she glanced down at her denim dress and wished she'd chosen the more flattering turquoise-colored silk instead.

"The table will be ready in a minute," Nick said, his hand lightly resting on her shoulder. "Can I get you anything from the bar?"

"No, thanks. I don't—"

"Taylor, over here."

Her heart caught in her throat. Even across the noisy room, she recognized Grandpa Bill's voice immediately.

"Nick." Another voice rang out from a far corner.

The arm around her shoulder tightened, and an expletive slipped past Nick's lips. A smile that didn't quite reach his eyes tipped the corners of his mouth, and he waved.

"Who's the guy headed this way?" he asked softly, talking through a smile, his breath warm against her ear.

"My grandfather." She glanced at the balding man barreling his way through the crowd. "Who's yours?"

"My soon-to-be business partner Henry Waters. His daughter, Claire, is the reason I need a fiancée." His fingers dug into her arm. "Smile."

"Just don't let on to my grandfather that I lost my job," she said under her breath.

What rotten luck! They hadn't even finished their first rehearsal and now they stood center stage. Apparently this was opening night, after all. She reached to push back a wayward strand of hair, and Nick grasped her hand, holding it tightly.

"Well, now, who do we have here?"

Nick turned in mock resignation to face the

knowing smile lingering on the lips of the large, middle-aged man.

"Henry, I didn't expect to see you here tonight."

"This must be your fiancée." The man chuckled. "At least I hope she is."

"Sweetheart, this is Henry Waters, the guy I've been telling you about. Henry, this is Taylor Rollins."

Nick cast her a sideways glance, and Taylor knew the moment had arrived. A split second to decide whether or not to take on the role.

"His fiancée," she said. "For now, anyway."

Nick's blue eyes flashed a gentle but firm warning. "Taylor and I can't wait for the wedding." He brought her hand to his mouth and caressed it with his lips. "Isn't that right, sweetheart?"

"Absolutely." She swallowed hard and smiled brightly. "Darling."

Henry stared, his dark eyes sharp and assessing. "Rollins, eh? Any relation to Bill?"

"I'm her grandfather."

"Bill, old buddy. I didn't see you." Henry extended his hand and slapped Taylor's grandfather on the back. "It's been a long time. How have you been?"

"Doing good." Bill cast a curious glance at Nick, who stood with his arm draped around Taylor's shoulders.

"I was just offering Nick and Taylor my congratulations," Henry said.

"Congratulations?"

"On their engagement. Don't tell me you didn't know."

"Of course I knew. I just didn't know they'd made the announcement public," her grandfather said smoothly, shooting Taylor a glance that told her she had some explaining to do.

"Nick told me earlier he'd proposed but wasn't sure of the answer. I don't mind admitting it took me by surprise. I'd always hoped he'd be my son-in-law someday. But I can blame my daughter for that. She left him alone too long. It was only natural he'd find someone else." Henry Waters rambled on, and Taylor shot a glance at Nick. His expression didn't change but his hand tightened on hers. "Anyway, that's water under the bridge. He certainly couldn't have done any better. Taylor seems like a lovely girl, and there's not a family in the state better thought of than yours, Bill."

"Nice of you to say, Henry."

Taylor swallowed hard against the lump in her throat. She'd made the right choice. No sacrifice would be too great if it preserved her father's reputation and her grandfather's health.

Her grandfather turned to Nick, and Taylor knew she should introduce the two, but Mr. Waters would wonder why Nick and Grandpa Bill had never met, and the whole deception would be over before it began.

"Son, it looks like congratulations are in order." For a moment Grandpa Bill studied Nick intently, and Taylor realized why he'd been so formidable in the courtroom. Nick returned the gaze steadily with a measuring one of his own until her grandfather smiled. "You'll have to come over to the house so we can formally welcome you to the family."

"Why don't you both join us for dinner?" Taylor said weakly, hoping they'd refuse.

Her grandfather shook his head. Regret laced his eyes. "I wish I could. But I'm here on business. In fact, we were just being seated when I caught a glimpse of you. And of course I had to come over."

"Of course." She smiled with relief, realizing again how much she loved this man. "I'll call you and Nana tomorrow."

"You do that." Her grandfather brushed a light kiss across her forehead, said his goodbyes and headed back to the dining room.

"Unfortunately I've got to get going, too." Henry clapped Nick on the back. "Jack Corrigan is over at the bar waiting."

Nick's face tightened. "I thought your negotiations with him ended when you accepted my offer."

"Jack and I are still old friends, Nick," Henry

said with a hint of reproof, "although I don't think he's quite forgiven me yet for picking Lanagan Associates over his company."

Nick's biceps tightened beneath her arm, but the smile he flashed epitomized confidence. "Friendship or not, he has to know you made the best choice. Be sure and tell him hello for me."

"I'll do better than that. I'll tell him to expect a wedding invitation. Any idea when the happy day will be?"

"No," Taylor said at the exact same moment Nick answered yes.

Henry laughed.

Nick smiled and shrugged. "We've tossed around a few dates, nothing definite yet. But I guarantee you'll be one of the first to know."

Taylor leaned back against Nick and kept a smile firmly in place until Henry Waters was out of sight. How was she ever going to pull this off?

Taylor slipped the key into the lock and turned to Nick. "The evening wasn't as bad as—"

"Before you stroke my ego with more kind words—" Nick's fingers slid sensuously up her arm "—I think it would be a good idea to seal this engagement with a kiss."

"Why would you think that?" Her heart picked up speed.

"We need the practice." Nick's tone was half

serious, half teasing. "And in case someone's watching."

Taylor laughed and glanced at a nearby tree. "Wave to Grandpa Bill."

Warm flesh closed over her hand, and the laughter died in her throat. Instinctively she tried to pull away, but his grip tightened.

"Okay, maybe he's not there tonight—" his lips brushed against her hair, as his other hand cupped her cheek "—but we still need the practice."

She shivered beneath his touch. Her heart pounded against the thin denim of her dress, but she didn't move.

His jaw relaxed, and he bent down, the warm smile more genuine now. His lips moved over hers, softly at first, as if testing the waters, then more firmly. Her arms unexpectedly wrapped around his neck.

Her heart pounded like a sledgehammer in her chest. More affected than she would ever admit, Taylor drew her head back and looked at this man she'd just kissed, this stranger, her temporary fiancé.

"Wow." He raised one dark brow. "That was some dress rehearsal."

He reached for her again, but Taylor shook her head and sidestepped his embrace. "I think we've practiced enough for one evening."

"Practice makes perfect." His heated gaze

searched her eyes, and he smiled so enticingly she had to look away or give in. "Are you sure?"

Of course she wasn't sure. But she was sensible. Not to mention responsible. "Positive."

"Just one more for the road?"

She smiled, giving him a solid A for effort. "Not tonight. But since we're engaged, I'm sure they'll—"

"Engaged." He shoved one hand into his pants pocket. "I'm glad you reminded me."

He pulled out a tiny velvet box and pushed it into her hand. "Here. You'll need this."

Her heart twisted. She'd dreamed about receiving an engagement ring. But never had she thought it would be like this.

"Aren't you going to open it?"

"Sure. Why not?" She snapped the box open and gasped. The large emerald-cut diamond in an antique setting had to be at least five carats. "This is way too much. I can't accept this."

"Sure you can," he said, removing the ring from its velvet nest and slipping it on her finger. "It was my grandmother's. Just remember, I want it back when we break up."

She glanced at the stone. "Gee, thanks, Romeo."

He ignored her sarcasm and reached for her hand, holding it up to the porch light. "It looks good on you, Juliet. I guess it's official. We're engaged."

"Temporarily," she murmured.

The gem caught the light's rays, and a prism of colors shot from its depths. A beautiful prop. A precious gem to grace her finger for the next three months before being returned to storage. An outward symbol of deception, not of love and commitment. Was this really the road she was meant to travel?

"What are you thinking?"

Taylor pulled her gaze from the ring and shoved her doubts aside. "I'm thinking I can hardly wait to see what happens in Act Two."

# Chapter Four

Nick leaned back in his leather desk chair and laced his fingers together behind his head. His gaze never left her face. "Mind telling me what's so important I had to leave a meeting that took me two weeks to arrange? The way you're acting, I can't imagine it's because you missed me."

It had been three days since she'd accepted his offer. Three days without so much as a phone call. Three days of offering excuse after excuse to her grandparents.

"The way I'm acting? How would you act if a man you've just introduced as your fiancé drops off the face of the earth, doesn't return—"

"I was out of town."

"I don't care if you were in China." Only death

would have been a valid excuse for ignoring her fifteen voice messages. "You could have called."

"I was busy." A sudden thin chill hung on to the edge of his words.

"Busy?" she said sarcastically. "Too busy to pick up the phone?"

She stalked to his desk, picked up the receiver and shoved it into his hand. "How many seconds out of your *busy* schedule would that little gesture have taken? Five? Three?"

His lips quirked upward.

"Don't you dare smile at me, mister. Not after what you've put me through." She refused to be appeased. "What was I supposed to say when my grandparents asked why I wasn't bringing you over to meet them? I can't bring him because I don't know where he is? I can't set up a time because he won't return my calls? I wish I had a quarter for every time your secretary told me you were unavailable."

His smile vanished, and he set the receiver down with a slow, controlled gesture. "That's her standard response to callers."

"Even your fiancée?"

He had the grace to look slightly embarrassed. "I must have forgotten to mention—"

It was all she could do not to scream in frustration. "Nick Lanagan, if I had a rope you would be swinging from the chandelier in the lobby right now.''

''What a romantic picture,'' a sultry voice purred.

Taylor's gaze jerked to the intruder in the doorway. The sleeveless white linen sheath emphasized the woman's deep rich tan, and the alligator belt around her waist accentuated her smallness. Her thick dark hair hung in long graceful waves over her shoulders.

''Although I must admit ropes don't do much for me. I've always been partial to satin sheets and champagne.''

Shocked, Taylor could only stare at the unknown woman.

''Claire.'' Nick rose from his chair and circled the desk to stand at Taylor's side. ''I'd like you to meet my fiancée, Taylor Rollins. Taylor—Claire Waters.''

So this was the infamous Claire. Taylor narrowed her gaze, a tiny, superficial smile tipping her lips. The woman was a barracuda. In the political arena such women were well known. It didn't matter if the man was married or engaged, he was fair game. Consequently Taylor had developed a deep distrust of such creatures.

Claire smiled and crossed the thick gray carpet, her hips swinging seductively. Her dark eyes glittered, sharp and assessing. "Do I detect trouble in Paradise?"

Nick laughed and slid his arm around Taylor's shoulders. "Just a little quarrel. In fact, if you hadn't interrupted we'd already be into the kissing and making-up stage."

"Don't let me stop you." Claire waved one hand, her cherry-red nails cutting a bright swath in the air. She sat in the corner wing chair, crossing one perfect leg over the other.

For a long moment Nick stood silent, and a tiny muscle twitched in his jaw. Then he turned and curled his finger under Taylor's chin, tipping her face to his. "I'm sorry I was so inconsiderate. Will you forgive me?"

Taylor nodded and shoved aside her irritation. Was this sincerity an act for his old girlfriend's benefit or was Nick truly sorry? With Claire watching their every move there was no way to be sure. Still, what could she do but lift her gaze and force a slight smile? "Yes. I'll forgive you."

As if on cue, Nick's mouth lowered to hers, leaving her no time to prepare.

She couldn't pull away.

She couldn't act repelled.

She couldn't do much of anything.

His lips covered hers, and for an instant all she *could* do was respond. Taylor jerked back, and a warmth crept up her neck. "Nick, not here. We have an audience."

Claire's brown eyes, so dark they were almost black, measured her with a cool, appraising look. Taylor lifted her chin and stared back, her fingers twisting the unfamiliar ring on her left hand. A plethora of blue sparks shot from the mounted gem, scattering the midday sun.

Claire's eyes widened, and an absurd sense of satisfaction swept through Taylor. She curved her fingers around Nick's arm, giving the other woman a clear view of the impressive jewel.

The slight smile that tipped Nick's lips told her the gesture hadn't gone unnoticed.

Claire's gaze moved slowly back and forth, studying Taylor's face for an extra beat before sending a brilliant smile in Nick's direction. "Daddy and I have decided to throw you an engagement party. Assuming, of course, you and—"

Her hand fluttered in the air as if trying to recall some insignificant fact.

"Taylor," Nick told her, and Taylor smiled at the amusement in his voice.

"Oh, yes. Taylor. Assuming, of course, that you two will still be together then."

"Don't worry about that." Nick chuckled, and his arm tightened around Taylor's waist. "This is the woman for me."

For a fraction of a second, Claire's face stiffened

then she shot him a sly smile. "If you're happy, I'm happy."

In a pig's eye, Taylor thought.

Claire reached into her bag and pulled out a notepad and pen. "I'll need your mother's current address so I can send her an invitation."

"Don't waste your stamp." Nick rounded the corner of the desk and hit his phone's do-not-disturb button.

"Now, Nick, I'm sure Sylvia loves your fiancée and would be crushed if she didn't have the opportunity to toast your engagement." Claire smiled brightly. "In fact, Daddy told me the cutest story yesterday and I said, 'Well, it sounds like Nick got himself a woman just like his mother!'"

Taylor shifted uneasily.

"You don't mind if I tell it, do you?" Claire's dark eyes flashed beguilingly at Taylor, her rosy lips turned up in a pouty smile.

"I'm not sure what story you're talking about," Taylor said.

"It's the one where you visited your grandparents for the summer and wouldn't wear the same outfit twice." Claire shot a slanted look to Nick as if to make sure he was listening. His smile remained, but his jaw was clenched. "Daddy said you maxed out your grandfather's credit card and then threw a fit at the mall when he told you no more clothes. It was the talk of Cedar Ridge for months. Sounds like your mother, doesn't it, Nick?''

His eyes narrowed, and Taylor shifted beneath his gaze. She remembered that time all too well. Her mother had died that spring, and her father had set off on the campaign trail. She'd been filled with resentment over being left behind. Grandpa Bill and Nana had borne the brunt of her teenage anger and angst that summer. ''I'm surprised he remembered. That was so long ago. I was barely sixteen.''

''But those are our formative years—aren't they?'' Claire smiled sweetly.

Taylor opened her mouth to respond, but Claire cut her off. ''I guess I always thought Nick was looking for a different kind of woman.''

An inexplicable look of withdrawal came over Nick's face. He remained silent, forcing Taylor to answer.

''He was,'' Taylor said. ''Me.''

''Of course,'' Claire murmured. Her lashes swept down across her cheekbones, covering the satisfied gleam in her eyes. ''Well, I need to scoot. Nick, I'll give you a call this week and we'll do lunch.''

''I'm not sure I can make it. But maybe you and Taylor can get together.''

''Sure.'' Irritation colored Claire's dark eyes but her smile never wavered. She grabbed her bag and rose. ''Daddy and I are meeting at eleven, and he'll have my head if I keep him waiting.''

The door couldn't close quickly enough behind her. Taylor breathed a sigh of relief.

"I don't think she bought it," Nick said, rubbing his chin, his gaze focused on the closed door.

"How could you tell?"

"She was way too nice."

"That was nice?" Taylor widened her eyes. "You're kidding, aren't you?"

"I wish I was," he said. "Seriously, she was being charming today."

"Charming? That wasn't quite the word I'd use. How could you ever have dated her?"

"We all make mistakes." Nick motioned for Taylor to sit. He leaned against the desk, his expression thoughtful. "Claire was one of mine. And a big one."

"I think she's still interested, engagement or no engagement. Why, she practically threw herself at you."

"I expected as much." He paused and searched Taylor's face, for what she wasn't sure. "That's why you're here. To run interference so I can get some work done. But you're going to need to loosen up. Relax a little. Otherwise, she'll never believe this engagement is real."

"I'm doing the best I can, but—"

"I'm not saying you don't show promise. The kiss was pretty good." He shot her an irresistibly devastating grin, and despite herself, her heart raced. "With a little practice, I think we could really nail it. And since we don't have an audience now…"

His smile widened and brought out the dimples in his cheeks. She really liked those dimples.

In another instant she would have been in his arms. But it was the self-satisfied gleam in his blue eyes as he stepped forward that brought her back to reality. She pulled her gaze from his and took a deep steadying breath, forcing herself to remember the reason for today's visit.

"Since we don't have an audience, we need to talk about you meeting my grandparents."

He stopped. His smile disappeared.

"Tonight," she added.

He leaned across the desk and flipped open his planner. His gaze lowered briefly before he shook his head. "Tonight's not good for me. I've—"

"Tonight," Taylor said firmly. "I'm not putting them off any longer. Pick me up at seven."

His lips tightened, and his eyes darkened dangerously. For a long moment she thought he'd refuse.

He snapped the appointment book shut. "Seven it is."

She could tell he was angry, but she ignored his scowl. "Nick?"

He looked up from the pile of papers in front of him. "Yes?"

"Don't forget to tell Miss Dietrich I'm your fiancée and she's to put me through when I call." Taylor's voice oozed with a syrupy sweetness at odds with the directness of her gaze.

"Consider her told." Nick's gaze never wavered, but for an instant, Taylor swore something that looked a lot like respect flickered in his eyes. "See you at seven."

Like actors with little in common except the performance, they headed their separate ways. Nick returned to his paperwork and Taylor pulled the door closed behind her.

With a little more effort on both their parts, this business arrangement could work. At the end of the summer she'd have her money and he'd have his merger. They'd go their separate ways and no one would be the wiser. No one would be hurt. It sounded reasonable. Then why did she have this sinking feeling that it wasn't going to be that simple?

Nick leaned back in the overstuffed sofa and took a sip of espresso. Taylor's grandmother—who'd insisted he call her Nana—sat a plate of tiny cookies on the table at his side.

His gaze slid over the festive platter, and he reached out and took a cookie. Nana's smile widened, and Taylor shot him an approving glance.

His temporary fiancée looked especially beautiful

this evening, Nick thought taking a bite and reflecting on his impulsive choice. The warm glow from the lamplight brought out the red in her hair, and her green eyes glittered like a pair of emeralds. He reached over and covered her hand with his, giving it a little squeeze.

The large diamond was hard against his palm, but he'd expected that. It was the coldness of her skin that surprised him. Obviously she was not as relaxed as she appeared. Perhaps she wasn't as easy to read as he'd first thought.

Keeping his hand in place, Nick turned to Bill Rollins, who thankfully hadn't insisted Nick call him anything but Bill. "Have you known Henry Waters long?"

"Actually..." Bill paused. "I've known Henry for almost thirty years. He and I have served on a couple of committees together and we've golfed in the same league for years. How about you?"

"We met at a Rotary Golf Scramble a couple of years ago," Nick said, thinking back to his first impression of Henry. He'd dismissed the man as a loud-mouthed blowhard who drank too much. Since then he'd realized that although his first impression was correct, there was a little more to the man than met the eye. A shrewd businessman, Henry was intensely loyal to his friends and his family. Nick sighed. Hence the problem with Claire.

"I didn't know you golfed." Taylor's voice

broke through his thoughts. It was a simple statement but Nick nearly groaned. Instead he smiled. "Sure you did, sweetheart. Remember we talked about going out to the Lodge sometime?"

Understanding filled her eyes. She laughed. A pleasant musical sound. "Of course...how could I have forgotten?"

Bill's eyes lit up, and he leaned forward in his chair. "If you're free on Friday morning, some friends and I get together for eighteen. We tee off at nine."

Nick could feel Taylor tense beside him. What was she so afraid of? That he'd bluntly turn the man down? If she knew him better, she'd realize he hadn't gotten where he was in the business world by alienating future contacts. He'd long ago learned the value of a tactful refusal.

Nick took a deep breath and mentally framed his answer.

"Grandpa, maybe Nick would like to know who else he'd be playing with." Taylor's voice was soft and low beside him.

"Of course, my dear." The smile Bill dispensed to his granddaughter was filled with love and indulgence. "You might even know them, Nick. Jack Corrigan and Tom Watts?"

A band tightened around Nick's chest, but he kept his voice offhand. "Jack and I have met. He was one of the bidders for Henry's company."

Bill's expression turned thoughtful. "I think I do remember hearing something about that. Jack had really counted on getting that bid."

*Just as I thought.*

No wonder old Corrigan was still cozying up to Henry. He was probably looking for an opening, any opportunity to get Henry to change his mind. Too bad he didn't realize he was wasting his time. There would be no opportunity. Nick would make sure of that. The refusal died on his lips. There might be some value in being a part of this foursome, after all.

"Fridays are usually good for me." The lie slipped easily from his lips.

Pleasure lit Bill's face, and Nick knew he'd scored some big points tonight. "We meet in the clubhouse for coffee at eight, if you'd like to join us?"

"Works for me." Nick smiled and slipped his arm around Taylor's shoulders. There just might end up to be more benefits to this arrangement than he'd ever dreamed.

Utterly drained, Taylor leaned her head against the leather headrest and closed her eyes.

The smooth ride of the Jag acted as a soothing balm on her frayed nerves. From the time they'd set foot in her grandparents' house, every fiber in her body had been on alert; the enormity of the task that loomed before her was mind-boggling. What ever made her think she could convince these two people who knew her better than anyone in the world she was in love with Nick? And he was in love with her? She would have bet there wasn't an actor alive who could pull off such a feat.

But she'd underestimated Nicholas Lanagan.

Again.

With a warm smile and an engaging manner, he'd set about convincing her grandparents he was a man in love. He was so good she almost believed him herself. She could see why he'd been so successful in his business.

"Nick, did you feel—I don't know—uncomfortable at all this evening?"

He chuckled. "Will you bite my head off if I say no?"

She heaved a heavy sigh. "They loved you. Your champagne toast brought tears to Nana's eyes."

"I'll take that as a compliment."

"I'm just worried—"

"You worry too much."

A year ago, worry and Taylor Rollins would never have been mentioned in the same breath. No one longed more for the carefree person she'd once been than she did. "I just hope they won't be too upset when we break up. They've been hurt enough for one lifetime."

"Losing their daughter-in-law and then their son, that would have been tough."

A chill filled the car that had nothing to do with the air conditioner. Her mother had been dead over ten years, but discussing her father's death still brought tears to her eyes. "It was horrible."

"Did your father and his parents have a close relationship?"

"He was their only son. The light of their life."

"You sound bitter."

"Do I? I don't mean to. I mean I'm not. My father was a great guy."

"Tell me about him."

"Why?"

"Your grandfather mentioned him several times. He seemed to assume I knew all about him."

"My grandpa obviously likes you. He doesn't talk about my father much anymore."

"He did to me."

"You played a convincing adoring fiancé." *Too convincing.* "That toast—how did you put it again—to the woman—"

"—who made me realize that I could have all the riches in the world but be poor without her by my side. And then I added that part about you being my best friend." He shot her a crooked grin. "Your grandparents seemed to find it very touching."

"You're incorrigible." Her lips tipped up in spite

of herself. No doubt about it, Nick had a certain romantic-hero type appeal.

*Actresses always fall in love with their leading men.*

Nonsense. She wasn't some naive Hollywood starlet. She was a responsible adult who knew the line between fiction and reality. She had a job to do. And as long as she remembered she was playing a role, she'd be just fine.

No matter how realistic the part.

No matter how handsome the leading man.

# Chapter Five

Nick eased the Jag into one of the last remaining spots in the gravel lot and shut off the engine. He removed the key but remained seated, his gaze shifting to the blue skies overhead.

The often unpredictable northeastern Colorado weather had cooperated. The temperature was balmy, and there wasn't a cloud in sight.

"You couldn't have picked a more beautiful day for a company picnic." Taylor tried to forget her apprehensions and enjoy the day. As a politician's daughter she'd faced similar situations many times. The fact that this time it would be Nick's colleagues who would be watching her, assessing her, shouldn't change a thing.

"Actually the date is picked a year in advance," Nick said. "That way everyone can plan ahead."

"Now that you mention it, I seem to recall when I was first hired seeing some information regarding a picnic in my welcome packet." Taylor remembered being told to set the date aside. "What's the big deal, anyway?"

Nick opened his **door**, got out and rounded the front of the car to open her door. "Just wait. You'll see."

He took her hand loosely in his. A surge of electricity shot up her arm and it was all she could do not to pull away.

Why did his presence affect her so much? Every time she was close to him, it was like being in junior high again. Her heart picked up speed, excitement surged up her spine and she felt as awkward as a teenager on her first date.

She'd never reacted so strongly to a guy she knew well, let alone one she'd barely met. Even Tony, who'd been her friend forever, had never caused the slightest tingle to travel up her spine.

But at twenty-six she was no unsure teen, and over the years she'd become proficient in concealing her emotions, especially troublesome ones. She smiled and let Nick help her out of the low-slung sports car, ignoring the subtle musky scent of his cologne.

They strolled down a mulch-strewn path leading into the park, and Taylor concentrated on the beauty of the surrounding woods. A ground squirrel darted in front of them.

Delighted, Taylor turned to Nick, lifting her face to his, one hand lightly touching his shoulder. "Did you—"

His lips lowered to hers, and suddenly the question no longer mattered. The kiss ended quickly. With a warm hand Nick brushed a strand of her hair from her face. It was a tender gesture. Her heart lurched. "That's better."

"Better?" Confusion clouded her thoughts. "What do you mean better?"

"You have that 'I've just been kissed' look." His gaze searched her face. "Now you look like a woman in love."

In love? She wanted to laugh, but a tightness filled her throat and she couldn't pull her gaze from his.

"On second thought…" A dimple flashed in his cheek, and once again his mouth lowered.

The sounds of the woods faded and Taylor lost herself in the warmth and sweetness of Nick's kiss. She wrapped her arms around his neck, and he pulled her close, his fingers hot against her back.

"All right, you two. Break it up." Taylor jerked back at the amused masculine voice. Or as far back as Nick's unyielding arms would allow. Unlike her, his only reaction to the intruder was to raise his head and shift his gaze in the direction of the sound.

"Erik." A hint of annoyance crossed Nick's face. "Shouldn't you be manning the grill or something?"

"I'd rather watch you." Erik leaned against the trunk of a tall tree, folded his arms across his chest and stared from Nick to Taylor with an innocent expression.

Taylor laughed. She couldn't help it. Although she'd only met Erik once or twice, her instincts told her that this behavior was classic Erik.

"Nick and I were just discussing the picnic," Taylor said, regretting the words the instant they left her mouth.

Nick raised a brow, his lips twitching.

This time it was Erik who laughed. "Don't tell me. Let me guess. We're going to have a kissing booth and Nick was just checking to see if you'd be worth a dollar a pop?"

"Erik," Nick growled.

Erik ignored him, and his gaze slid up and down Taylor's form. For a second she wondered if her jeans were too tight or if the sleeveless cotton top clung too closely to her curves. They'd passed muster in the full-length mirror at home, but under Erik's intense scrutiny she wasn't so sure.

"I'd be glad to help out with the research." Erik reached for Taylor's arm. "Give a second opinion."

"Don't even try it." Nick's lips curved in a smile, but the warning in his blue eyes was clear.

Erik's hand dropped to his side, but instead of being upset at his friend, his amusement seemed to be even more pronounced. "All right, have it your way."

"Did we get a good crowd?" Nick moved his arm so her hand slid down to his, and he gently locked his fingers with hers before starting down the path with Erik following behind.

"You bet." Erik's voice was filled with satisfaction. "Miss Dietrich even showed up this year."

Nick stopped suddenly and turned to his friend. "She did?"

Taylor shot a questioning glance at Nick.

"She hasn't come since my father died," he said simply.

"Well, I for one wish she'd stayed away." Erik heaved an exaggerated sigh. "She's been hounding me for the last twenty minutes about when we're going to eat."

"Hounding?" Nick's expression was clearly skeptical.

"All right," Erik said. "Maybe she just said something about making sure the meat didn't get too done, but I know what she meant."

Guilt washed over Taylor. They'd been late because of her.

"Sweetheart." The word still felt awkward on

her lips. "If people are waiting we'd better get going."

"You're right." Nick smiled but made no move to go. Instead he lowered his mouth to hers one last time.

Taylor resisted the urge to sidestep his kiss. She'd never been comfortable with public displays of affection, and Erik made no attempt to look away. But she had a role to play, and making the engagement seem real was part of it.

"Nick." Erik cleared his throat. "Think about the meat."

Nick's thoughtful gaze lingered for a moment longer, then he smiled. "Now I'm ready."

The picnic was unlike any Taylor had ever attended. She'd expected the long rows of tables covered with red and white cloths, overflowing with salads to satisfy any and all tastes. The chips were there, too, along with the roasted sweet corn and watermelon. It took three tables to handle all the pies, and Taylor's mouth watered at the sight of a pumpkin pie with pecan streusel topping.

But Nick pulled her past the beckoning tables, past the people standing in small groups staring with unabashed interest and past a stern-faced Miss Dietrich.

They stopped abruptly before a raised platform, and Nick gestured for Taylor to climb the two small steps to the stage.

She stood on the raw plywood, and Nick moved quickly to her side. Within seconds, the people who'd been milling around surrounded them. Everyone *had* been waiting for Nick to arrive. Her guilt intensified.

Nick turned on the charm the minute he began speaking, starting with a joke about why they were late and ending with the announcement they'd all anticipated.

"You all know how much this company means to me. I never thought I'd find anything that mattered as much to me. Well, I was wrong. When I met Taylor Rollins, it was no contest. And, although we'll be formally announcing our engagement in a few weeks, I wanted all of you to be the first to know." Nick pulled her to his side and grinned.

The crowd cheered, and Taylor pasted what she hoped was a properly adoring expression on her face.

The look of approval he shot her told her she'd hit the mark. He captured her hand with his, and from the broad smile on his face, he looked perfectly relaxed. But his hand gripped hers a little too tightly, and a barely perceptible muscle in his jaw jumped.

She'd grown up with a supremely confident male who never let on if he had worries or concerns. Knowing that this wasn't easy for Nick, either, made her feel closer to him. Impulsively, she turned and kissed him lightly on the mouth.

Surprise flickered in his eyes. He responded immediately. He tugged her toward him.

"Nick—"

He stopped her words by covering her mouth with his. It was an exquisite kiss and it made her forget for a brief moment in time that she stood center stage with hundreds of people watching.

The crowd roared their approval.

Nick released her, an odd tender look in his eyes. Taylor caught her breath and waved to the employees and their families.

Off to the side, Miss Dietrich stood, her arms folded across her chest, staring intently.

"Let's eat," Nick said.

As if on cue everyone scattered toward the food-laden tables.

Taylor's shoulders slumped in relief. The hard part was over.

Nick gave her hand a squeeze. "You did good."

"I don't think I'm cut out for this," she said with a sigh. "My stomach is churning."

"That's because—" he gently took her arm "—you're hungry. Come with me."

He pulled her toward the tantalizing scent of barbecue. A huge metal smoker loomed before them, and Taylor realized where Erik had disappeared to once they'd reached the picnic ground. Resplendent in a chef's hat and apron, the young attorney stood dishing out platters of ribs and barbecued beef.

Taylor's mouth started to water and she had to concede that maybe Nick was right. Maybe she was just hungry.

"Mr. Lanagan." A man Taylor remembered vaguely from her brief time at the company stopped them. "I hate to interrupt but could I speak with you a minute?"

Nick hesitated, and she knew he was remembering his promise to not desert her.

"Go ahead." She smiled. "I'll be fine."

Taylor took her place in line and filled her plate to the point of overflowing. She balanced it carefully in one hand, gripping a tall plastic cup of iced tea in the other.

The picnic tables were rapidly filling, and Taylor glanced around looking for a place to squeeze in.

"You're welcome to join me, if you like." The perfectly modulated voice sounded from her right.

Taylor turned and met the formidable gaze of Miss Dietrich. Her stomach clenched. They'd barely exchanged ten words since they'd met, but the woman still intimidated her. She was set to politely decline the offer, but something in the older woman's look and the fact that the secretary sat alone at the end of the bench while others seemed to be surrounded by family and co-workers changed her mind.

"Thanks." Taylor carefully lowered her plate and cup to the table's rough surface, then slid onto the bench opposite the woman.

She dropped a paper napkin onto her lap and lifted her gaze to find Miss Dietrich staring unabashedly.

Startled, Taylor shifted her gaze and popped a chip in her mouth.

Miss Dietrich hesitated for a second then grabbed a chip from her own plate and took a bite. "The sour cream and onion are my favorite."

The tenseness in Taylor's shoulders eased. Away from the domain of her office, the woman actually seemed pleasant. Maybe this wasn't going to be as bad as she'd thought.

Taylor picked up another chip, holding it loosely in her fingers. "You've known Nick for a long time, haven't you?"

"Since he was a little boy," Miss Dietrich said matter-of-factly. "I was his father's secretary for over twenty years."

"What was he like?" Though the barbecued beef on her plate beckoned, the desire to learn more about Nick overpowered her appetite.

"Nick? Or his father?"

"Nick," Taylor said immediately, then realized although she knew very little about her temporary fiancé, she knew next to nothing about his family. "Both."

Miss Dietrich dabbed the corners of her mouth with the edge of her napkin. "Nick was a sweet, serious little boy. He adored his father."

"It sounds like they were very close."

"As close as they could be." Miss Dietrich took a sip of her tea. "Nick's father faced a daunting task. When he started out, computers were in their infancy. There were constant changes in the field and Nick's father was determined to be at the forefront. Consequently he spent a lot of time at the office."

"But what about Nick and his mom? Where did they fit into his life?"

Miss Dietrich's gaze turned disapproving, as if Taylor had uttered an obscenity. "Mr. Lanagan was a good man. He did—"

"My two favorite ladies." Nick grinned and slid next to Taylor, his arm reaching up to rest loosely around her shoulder. "You both look so serious. What's up?"

An uncomfortable look flashed across the older woman's face, and she pursed her lips.

Taylor shifted her gaze and her breath caught in her throat. If she had to play this part, she couldn't have picked a more handsome leading man. She forced her thoughts to the conversation. "Miss Dietrich was just telling me about your father's accomplishments. It sounds like he was a remarkable man."

"He was." Nick nodded. "He was the reason Lanagan Associates flourished. It took a lot of time and effort, but to him, it was worth it. The company wasn't just his job, it was his life."

The question that Miss Dietrich hadn't answered still nagged at her. Taylor frowned. "But what about you and your mom?"

Nick shrugged and grabbed a potato chip from her plate. "We understood. Or at least I did. Dad always said for a business to be a success, it has to come before anything else in a man's life."

Taylor nodded as if what he'd said made perfect sense instead of being the antithesis of everything she believed. She wanted to ask him if he felt that way, too. But the thought of putting him on the spot before his employee kept the words from her lips.

And what did it matter anyway? She wasn't marrying the man. When she really did get married it would be to a man who shared her beliefs and values. A man who put God and family before his career. A man who loved her with his whole heart.

Taylor cast a sideways glance and sighed. And maybe if it wasn't too much to ask and she was really lucky, that man would be as handsome as Nick Lanagan.

# *Chapter Six*

~~~

Taylor hung up the phone and heaved a sigh of relief. Since the picnic Nick had been extremely busy at work and he hadn't been able to fit any "together" time into his schedule. She'd wondered how he'd react to her invitation to attend church with her and her grandparents on Sunday. Would he refuse to go? Or see it for what it was? A way to convince her grandparents that this engagement was the real thing. Thankfully, he'd agreed to go.

Nana and Grandpa Bill hadn't wasted any time telling Pastor Schmidt about her engagement, and she'd been shocked to discover that the pastor had recently spoken to Nick. According to the minister, Nick was currently in the process of transferring his membership from a Denver congregation and was anxious to get involved with some of the standing committees. She'd had to smile and act as if she knew all about it.

Her grandfather had beamed at the news and made sure the pastor knew that the finance committee he chaired could use another member.

Taylor leaned back against the sofa, her mind a jumbled mass of confusing thoughts and feelings. As happy as she was to hear about Nick's interest in the church, something didn't ring true. If he was so interested in church, why had he insisted they attend the early service so "only the morning would be wasted"?

She'd had to bite her tongue. Praising God wasn't ever a waste of time, but how Nick led his life wasn't her business. He was her employer. Maybe once she knew him better, she could subtly mention he might want to look at his priorities.

Once she knew him better?

She chuckled at the thought, a twinge of sadness underlying her amusement. Nick was a stranger. And she needed to remember that by the time she got to know him better, he'd be history.

Nick hung up the phone, unable to keep an irritated scowl from his lips.

He'd made his obligatory daily call to Taylor. As he'd told Erik, a phone call was a small price to pay to keep in touch and head off any unforeseen problems before they developed. And it didn't take a lot of time. After all, what was five minutes in the total scheme of things? If he called from the office, he could still be productive and review his e-mail or sign some checks while she talked.

Not that he didn't like Taylor or enjoy her company. And he especially liked kissing her. At the picnic there had been absolutely no reason for him to kiss her in front of Erik. Erik knew the score, knew the engagement was a sham. Nick didn't need to make a point. The simple truth was he did it for the pure enjoyment.

His gaze slid to the picture of her that now graced the top of his desk. She'd stopped by the day after the dinner with her grandparents and left it for him, along with a note. She'd been right on target, and he wondered why he hadn't thought of it. Surely, a man would have a picture of his fiancée somewhere in his office.

His lips tilted upward in a smile. The picture was a good one, but then, he reminded himself, Taylor was a beautiful woman.

Is that why he'd said yes to her request? Because she was beautiful? Or because deep down he'd really wanted to see her again?

All he knew was, when she'd mentioned church, his gaze had shifted momentarily from his computer screen with its endless e-mail messages to her picture, lingering on those full lips, and he'd found himself saying yes, he'd accompany her and her grandparents on Sunday.

Thankfully, he'd retained enough of his good sense to insist they attend the early morning service. Going to the late one almost guaranteed that not only his morning but the whole day would be wasted.

Eventually he would get to know the members of this congregation better and the time would be well spent. As his father used to say, church was a good way of making new contacts and of strengthening the old. His mother would always bristle, insisting that that was not the purpose of church. His father paid her no mind. He'd just laugh, slap Nick on the back and make some comment about women not having a head for business.

Sylvia may not have understood business but she certainly understood how to spend money. Nick's lips tightened. Lots of money. So much that the company had been on the verge of bankruptcy by the time Nick had taken over.

A familiar bitterness welled deep inside Nick. She should have spent more time tending to his father's needs when he was sick rather than dragging him to all those parties. And each time with a new designer dress or some ostentatious piece of jewelry bought specifically for the occasion.

According to the housekeeper, his parents had fought continuously about money that last year.

Away at college, Nick heard all about it from the housekeeper, a woman intensely loyal to his father. She'd had nothing good to say about Sylvia Lanagan's behavior.

Nick's heart ached with sympathy for his father. He'd come home as often as he could, but he'd been a senior that year and it hadn't been near enough. If only he could have seen what was happening. If only...

Nick shoved aside the nonproductive thoughts. He had no time to waste on regrets. Only one thing was important—the merger with Waters Inc. Nothing else mattered. Nothing else was worth a second thought.

The door to Nick's office swung open. He spoke without looking up. "Just put the folders on the counter, Miss Dietrich."

"The old hag is down the hall at the copy machine."

The feminine voice was all too familiar. Nick could barely hide his groan. "Claire, I'm kind of busy here."

The overpowering scent of musk drew close. Nick kept his gaze on the troubling report from his new product chief.

Claire snatched the paper out of his hands. He jerked it back and glared at her.

She laughed, a pleased expression blanketing her carefully made-up face. "Still the same old Nick."

"Who else would I be?" This time he didn't even try to hide his irritation.

"I don't know." She pressed one finger to her lips and tilted her head as if pretending to think. "Maybe a love-struck fool?"

"Give it up, Claire."

She settled into the soft leather of the chair and looked at him innocently. "I'm just trying to make conversation. No need to bite my head off."

His fingers tightened around the edge of the desk. What was there about Claire Waters that pushed all his buttons?

"You're awfully cranky today. Are you and the girlfriend not getting along?" Her gaze turned sharp and assessing.

"Her name is Taylor," Nick said bluntly. "And for your information we're getting along just fine."

Claire twirled a strand of dark hair slowly around one finger. "If you say so."

He blew out a breath and gave in to the inevitable. Nick shoved the papers aside and leaned back in his chair. "Five minutes. You can have five minutes."

For the first time since she'd walked through his office door, Claire let some irritation show. Her dark eyes shot sparks, but her voice was well controlled. "You're an arrogant jerk, Nick Lanagan. No wonder I find you so appealing."

Nick raised a brow. "The clock's ticking. You've got three minutes."

"All right." Claire leaned forward in her chair. "Daddy was going to call you but I said I'd stop by and ask you personally. He wants you to meet us for breakfast Sunday morning. Some guy that heads his operations area in New Jersey is going to be in town."

A surge of excitement swept through Nick. After all these years, it was finally coming together. The Waters Inc. data warehousing operation would soon be his, and this meeting with Henry's operations chief only confirmed the reality. Sunday couldn't come soon enough.

*Sunday.*

His stomach twisted in a knot.

"Sunday morning's not good." He offered Claire his most engaging smile, wishing he'd been nicer to her earlier. "How about in the afternoon?"

"He's leaving at noon."

Nick raked his fingers through his hair. "I can make it any other time."

"That's the only time he's available." Claire rose effortlessly from the chair. "What's the problem? If I know you, it can't be because you want to sleep late."

Sleep late? There hadn't been a day in the last four years that he'd risen past seven.

If only his reason could be that simple. Bill Rollins might understand him skipping church, but he'd promised Taylor... Nick brought himself up short. Why was he so worried about her? She worked for him. He didn't owe her anything, least of all an explanation.

"On second thought, Sunday morning will work." Nick pushed back his chair, stood and rounded the desk. He gestured toward the door. "Let Miss Dietrich know the time and place on your way out."

Instead of heading toward the door, Claire moved closer. So close the overpowering scent of her perfume surrounded him. So close it took only one simple movement for her to reach up and pull his face to hers. For her mouth to meet his. Her lips were warm with a hint of promise.

And left him cold.

"Mr. Lanagan." Miss Dietrich's disapproving voice sounded from the doorway.

"Yes, Miss Dietrich?" Nick took a step back. He resisted the urge to brush away the taste of Claire from his lips with the back of his hand.

Claire smiled brightly at the secretary, her expression filled with satisfaction. At that moment Nick could see why Erik called her Catwoman. She looked like a cat that had just swallowed a canary.

Disapproval radiated from every inch of Miss Dietrich's ramrod stiff posture. The older woman's gaze slid dismissively over Claire before meeting Nick's head-on. "Your fiancée called."

Nick cleared his throat and forced an interested smile. "Did she leave a message?"

"I told her you were in conference. She wanted you to call when you were free."

"Miss Waters is just leaving." He'd done nothing wrong, so why did he feel like he had?

Claire ran a long red fingernail up his sleeve. "But we were just getting started."

Nick leveled her a warning glance. "Goodbye, Claire."

She hesitated then shrugged. "I've got some business to take care of anyway." Claire's lofty gaze settled on the secretary. "Mr. Lanagan is meeting me at nine a.m. on Sunday at the Heritage Hotel. Be sure and put it on his calendar."

Her request was imperious and clearly designed to put Miss Dietrich in her place.

It didn't work.

Miss Dietrich drew herself up to full stature and turned with a disdainful sniff.

Shocked, Claire's eyes widened. Nick hid a grin behind his hand. Claire would soon learn that no one got the best of Miss Dietrich. Not even Henry Waters's little princess.

Impatiently, Nick shifted in the high-backed wooden chair and wondered if it would be rude to leave. They'd started talking business the second he'd sat down, rather than wasting time in idle chitchat. He appreciated that fact since the purpose of the meeting was business, not social. But now the talk had turned personal, and bored stiff with the aimless chatter, Nick turned his attention to his surroundings.

The Pioneer Room of the historic Heritage Hotel had been recently remodeled and no expense had been spared. The rustic wagon-wheel motif had been replaced by more elegant appointments that few early settlers would have recognized. Stained glass depicting life in the old west topped each window, and original prints and artwork from the era were strategically placed along the walls.

Nick waved away another cup of coffee and glanced down the table, noting the linen tablecloth, the sterling silverware and the crystal glasses. Fine china replaced the rustic glazed mugs favored by the previous owners.

The waitress removed the last of the empty plates, and Nick couldn't have said what he'd eaten. Jack Corrigan's unexpected presence at the table when he'd arrived had effectively killed his appetite.

Clint Donovan, Henry's operations chief, sat with Jack on the other side of the table, while Claire sat between Nick and Henry. All through the meal

Claire had rubbed her foot up the side of his pant leg. He'd done his best to ignore her.

"Nick, how's that beautiful fiancée of yours doing?" Jack added two spoonfuls of sugar to his coffee and took a sip.

"Great." Nick's smile was genuine. Taylor had surprised him and been a real trooper about the change in plans. Of course, he'd met her more than halfway by offering to call her grandparents and explain about the meeting.

"Fiancée?" Clint quirked a brow.

"Nick is engaged to Taylor Rollins." Jack explained before Nick could answer. "Her father was Robert Rollins, the senator who died in that car accident last year."

Clint glanced from Claire to Nick, a puzzled frown on his face. "But I thought you two…"

Nick's jaw clenched. "Claire and I were dating at one time. She left town. I met Taylor. The rest is history."

Clint shifted his openly curious gaze to Henry.

"I made no secret of the fact that I hoped my Claire and Nick would end up together." Henry heaved a sigh. "But I can't blame him. She had to go take that job in D.C."

Claire ignored her father's censuring glance and leaned across the table. She crooked a finger to Clint. He leaned forward. In a conspiratorial whisper, Claire spoke just loud enough for everyone at the table to hear. "What Daddy is trying to say is Taylor got him on the rebound."

Nick took a deep breath and counted to ten.

Claire smiled. Although she spoke to Clint, her gaze never left Nick's face. "I've tried to tell him now that I'm back he doesn't have to settle for second best."

"Claire!" Henry exclaimed.

Jack Corrigan choked on his coffee.

Clint quirked a brow.

Nick's hands clenched into fists, and he forced a laugh. "I don't think anyone who ever met Taylor would consider her a second-choice kind of woman, Claire."

Claire shrugged and sipped her mimosa.

"It must have been hard to lose the contract." Clint turned to Jack in an obvious effort to change the subject and make up for his earlier gaffe. "Those bids were so close."

It was all Nick could do not to groan out loud. Of all the topics for the man to pick, why did he have to choose that one?

The uneasy tension that had settled over the table thickened.

"So I understand," Jack said with an easy smile. "But that was Henry's call."

*Henry's call.*

Nick could tell that even now Jack didn't understand why he'd lost the bid. After all, Jack and

Henry were friends from way back. What would have made him choose Nick?

Claire's hand on his thigh reminded him of the answer. Keeping a smile on his face, Nick reached under the white linen and captured her wrist, effectively stopping the upward migration of her fingers.

A twinkle of amusement flashed in Claire's eyes, and she blew him a kiss. Henry's gaze turned sharp and assessing. A glimmer of hope reflected in their dark beady depths.

Nick pretended not to notice. He lifted his coffee cup with his free hand and nonchalantly took a sip of the lukewarm brew.

He'd been right all along. Henry *had* chosen Lanagan Associates because he hoped Nick would one day be his son-in-law. Now Henry valued his reputation too much to back out of the deal without having a valid business reason. But if Nick should become involved again with Claire, all bets were off.

Nick downed the last of the cold coffee and settled back in his chair. As long as he kept this fake engagement on track and Claire at bay, at the end of the summer everything would be just as he planned. Waters Inc. would be his.

# *Chapter Seven*

"**I** can't believe I let you talk me into this," Nick muttered and jammed his hands into his pockets.

"Will you relax?" Taylor snapped. "You look like you're headed to the gas chamber instead of a premarital counseling session."

"Same difference." Nick shook his head, and his dark hair glistened in the fluorescent light. "I can't believe I agreed to this."

"You already said that." Taylor took a deep breath and tried to slow her rapidly beating heart. Did he think this was easy on her? She'd known Pastor Schmidt since she was a child. And ever since her grandparents had surprised her by registering her and Nick for these classes, Taylor had been worried sick that the minister would see right through their sham engagement.

The door to the church office burst open. Taylor's and Nick's heads turned as one. A skinny blond woman with puffy bangs pulled a young man with glasses and a bad case of acne into the waiting room.

"C'mon, Tom." High and shrill, the young woman's voice grated on Taylor's already tightly strung nerves. "We're late."

"Mandy." Tom jerked his hand from hers. "Quit pullin' on me."

The irritation in his voice came through loud and clear. The blonde stopped suddenly and turned, her eyes wide with disbelief. Her lower lip, the pink lipstick half-chewed off, trembled.

"Oh, baby." The boy stepped toward her, his voice gentle and filled with concern. "Don't cry."

She sniffed loudly, and he hurriedly pulled a rumpled tissue from his pants pocket.

Taylor and Nick exchanged amused glances.

But Mandy wasn't through. Big tears welled in her blue eyes, and her bottom lip protruded further.

Taylor hid a smile. If she wasn't mistaken, Mandy had crying on demand down to an art form. She braced herself for a sob fest.

The door to Pastor Schmidt's office opened, effectively staving off the impending flood. Taylor offered up a prayer of thanks, and she and Nick rose to their feet as the minister entered the doorway.

"Welcome." The gray-haired minister smiled and stepped aside, motioning the four of them into his office. "We're a small group this evening, so we should all get to know each other really well."

Nick groaned under his breath. Taylor jabbed him in the ribs.

She ignored Nick's pained gasp and moved forward to greet the pastor. It was only with the help of God and Pastor Schmidt that she'd been able to survive the death of her father. Every time she'd thought she couldn't go on, he'd been there with words from the scripture to remind her that she wasn't alone.

"Pastor." Her smile was filled with genuine warmth. "I don't believe you've met Nick."

"Only over the phone," the minister said with a smile.

She introduced the two, and they shook hands.

"I've known Taylor since she was a little girl." Taylor squirmed under the approval in the pastor's eyes and wondered if he would smile with the same degree of fondness if he knew that her engagement was all a lie.

She squared her shoulders. She had a good reason for agreeing to this arrangement and she doubted that given the whole story even the good pastor could find fault with her motives. Plus, if she played this right, he'd never know.

As if he could sense her unease, Nick's arm slid

up to rest briefly around her shoulders, and he offered her that heart-stopping grin she found increasingly hard to resist.

Taylor's tension melted away under the heat of his gaze and when his hand moved down to take hers she didn't resist.

They followed Tom and Mandy into the study with the minister bringing up the rear.

Once they were all inside, Pastor Schmidt shut the door and gestured toward a semicircle of chairs.

Nick waited for her to take her seat before sitting down next to her.

"Okay." The minister rubbed his hands together and paced the room. "Let's get started."

Taylor listened in horror as he described the agenda for the next six Together Forever premarital sessions. This was going to be harder than she thought. The minister seemed to be into everyone sharing their thoughts and feelings. She'd hoped for more of a lecture format.

"Nick, why don't you start by telling us what first attracted you to Taylor?" Pastor Schmidt leaned back in his chair, an expectant look on his face.

Nick paused, and his gaze shifted to study Taylor for a moment. She held her breath and smiled encouragingly.

"It was her spirit." Nick's gaze didn't waver. "She's one determined woman. I admire that."

Heat rose up her neck and into her cheeks. Though she and Nick had gone out many times during the past few weeks, their conversations had remained light and superficial.

"Taylor?" The pastor raised a brow.

What had first attracted her to Nick? She remembered how he'd looked when she first saw him. Like a *GQ* model in a hand-tailored suit.

"He was so handsome." The truth popped out before she could stop it.

Mandy laughed, a childish giggle of a laugh.

Taylor cheeks grew hotter.

"Okay." The minister's lips twitched, and he shifted his gaze. "Mandy?"

"What first attracted me to Nick?" Mandy giggled again. "Or to Tom?"

Nick's cough sounded more like a chuckle, and Taylor bit her lip to keep from laughing.

Pastor Schmidt didn't answer. He shot the young woman the same penetrating gaze he'd used when someone had gotten out of line in confirmation class.

Mandy straightened in her chair and cleared her throat. "What attracted me first to my Tommy boy?"

Nick rolled his eyes, and Taylor shifted her gaze to the ceiling and bit her lip again to keep from laughing out loud.

Once she started, the young woman wouldn't

shut up. By the time Mandy finished her lengthy discourse on all of Tom's wonderful attributes, a hint of exasperation stole across Pastor Schmidt's normally jovial expression.

Thankfully, Mandy had taken so long that Tom had plenty of time to contemplate his answer, and he took only seconds to murmur something about Mandy's generous, fun-loving personality.

Mandy's face filled with pleasure, and Taylor found her irritation lessening.

"We've got a good group here," Pastor Schmidt said. "I think we're going to work well together."

Taylor smiled and nodded as if she understood, even though she didn't. Other than motormouth Mandy, the rest of them had barely said five words. How could he possibly know if they'd work well together or not? Still, if the minister wanted to be an optimist, who was she to be a naysayer?

Like a coach trying to rev up his players before a big game, the minister launched into a sermon on Christian love and commitment. Taylor leaned back in her chair and relaxed. This was more like what she'd expected. He'd talk and they'd listen.

"At the end of each session, you'll be given a homework assignment."

Taylor straightened in her chair and shot Nick an incredulous look. "Homework?" she mouthed.

Nick shrugged.

"I want you to discuss what each partner expects from the other in a marriage."

"You mean like who should mow the yard? That kind of thing?" Mandy's brows furrowed.

"We could make a list," Tom added enthusiastically.

"No. I'm not talking about the day-to-day concerns, although those are important." The minister smiled. "I'm talking in terms of what role Christ and His church will play in your married life."

Mandy opened her mouth, but the minister waved her silent. "I'm not going to say any more. I want to leave it as open-ended as possible."

"Pastor." Mandy raised her hand like a child in school. "I have a question, but it's not about our homework."

"Yes, Mandy?"

"Why did you ask me what I liked about Tom?" Clearly puzzled, Mandy's thin features creased into a frown. "You asked all of us and then we didn't talk about it anymore."

That's because you talked about it enough for all of us, Taylor wanted to say. But a small part of her understood where Mandy was coming from. Taylor, too, had wondered what the minister had intended with that exercise.

"We were going to talk about it more when we meet in two weeks, but since you brought it up..." Pastor Schmidt paused. "Next time I'll ask you what made you first think you might be in love with your fiancé. The session after that there will be another relationship topic. Hopefully, by the end the reason for all the questions will be clear. I'd say more but I don't want to give the purpose away.''

Forestalling any further discussion, the minister ushered them out of his office. ''Don't forget the homework. Mandy, what do you expect from Tom? Taylor, what do you expect from Nick? And, vice versa.''

Taylor cast a sideways glance at Nick. What did she expect from him? Five thousand dollars a week and an uneventful engagement was all she asked. Hardly the stuff dreams are made of, but then she hadn't dreamed much in the last year.

Once her father's debts were paid off, her life would be her own again, and then maybe, one day, she could attend these classes again. This time with a man who loved her.

''Nick.'' Instead of immediately sliding into the convertible, Taylor paused at the open door. ''Thanks again for coming tonight.'' Her lips quirked. ''I know that when we discussed the terms of our engagement, premarital counseling wasn't mentioned.''

''Neither was the company picnic,'' Nick said with an easy smile.

''Do you have time to stop for coffee?'' For some reason, Taylor wasn't ready for the evening to end. "We could get our homework out of the way."

Nick paused as if seriously considering her invitation before he shook his head. "I can't. I have some proposals that I need to review before tomorrow. I'll be up half the night as it is."

"We'd better get going then." Taylor shoved aside her disappointment and reminded herself spending unnecessary time having coffee wasn't part of their business arrangement, either.

A loud curse echoed across the parking lot.

Taylor frowned and glanced over the concrete expanse.

Nick shifted his gaze to the only other car in the deserted lot. The vehicle was small and shaped like a tennis shoe with an oxidized yellow exterior highlighted by blotchy patches of rust.

"Isn't that Tom and Mandy?"

"Looks like they need some help." Despite his words about the work waiting at home, Nick didn't hesitate. He headed across the pavement with long purposeful strides, and Taylor had to run to keep up with him.

"Is the Gremlin dead?" Mandy's worried voice wafted on the breeze.

"It's not dead." Tom's muffled voice sounded from under the hood. "But the battery sure is."

"Can I help?" Nick stopped next to Tom. His

gaze shifted to the grease-covered motor, and his head joined Tom's under the hood.

Taylor stood on her tiptoes and peered over Nick's shoulder. She glanced at his intense expression. Did Nick know anything about engines?

"It's the battery." In the waning light, Tom looked young and defeated. His glasses had slipped down his nose, and he pushed them back with a grease-covered finger. "Couldn't have come at a worse time."

"Do you have any cables? We could try to jump it."

Tom shook his head.

"There's an auto parts store a couple of blocks from here. You can pick up a battery there." Nick glanced at his watch. "They should still be open. I can give you a lift."

Tom shifted uncomfortably. "Fact is I don't have the money for a new one right now. But if you could maybe give us a ride?"

Taylor's heart went out to the boy. She wished she could offer him the money, but the twenty dollars she had on her had to last until her next fiancée payment.

"Don't worry about it." Nick clapped a hand on the young man's back. "I have some extra cash I can lend you. You can pay me later."

Pride warred with relief on Tom's face. Finally

he nodded. "Thanks. I can pay you on the fifteenth, if that's okay?"

"That'd be fine," Nick said, and Taylor knew he didn't care if the young man paid him back or not.

Taylor shifted her gaze to the Jag. "Why don't Mandy and I just wait here? It's a little tight in that back seat."

"Is that your car?" Tom followed Taylor's gaze and gave a low whistle. "What is it?"

"Jaguar," Nick said. "An XK8."

Taylor and Mandy followed the guys over to the shiny silver-blue sports car.

"Twelve cylinders?" Tom ran his hands appreciatively over the sleek surface.

"V-eight," Nick said. "Thirty-two valves."

"Wow." Tom's eyes widened. "I bet it's fast."

"Zero to sixty in less than seven seconds."

"Unbelievable."

Taylor looked at Mandy, and they both smiled. Cars and sports seemed to be the universal language of men.

"Are you sure you don't want to ride with us?" Nick cast Taylor a questioning gaze.

"We'll be fine." She smiled reassuringly. "It's a beautiful night and this is a safe neighborhood. After all—" she gestured toward the church and the adjoining parsonage "—God is right next door."

Nick brushed a quick kiss across her lips and opened the car door. "Let's go."

He didn't have to ask twice. Tom couldn't get in the car fast enough. "I wish the guys at work could see me now."

The young man laced his fingers together behind his head and stretched back against the ivory-colored leather. "Man, is this livin' or what?"

Mandy giggled. Taylor smiled.

The engine roared to life and in a matter of seconds the car left the parking lot and sped off down the street.

Mandy waved until they were out of sight, then dug into her oversize purse and pulled out a tattered pack of chewing gum. "Want some?"

Taylor shook her head. "No, thanks."

"Let me know if you change your mind." Mandy shoved three pieces into her mouth and dropped the pack into her bag. "Want to go sit in the car?"

Taylor shrugged. "Okay."

Compared to the Jag, the Gremlin looked like a poor relative that was on its last leg. The passenger door stuck, and Mandy had to open it from the inside. She cleared some food wrappers from the seat and tossed them into the back of the car. "We drove through and got take-out on the way here."

Taylor smiled and brushed a French fry to the

floor before she sat down. "So when are you and Tom getting married?"

"October thirty-first."

Taylor turned in her seat, not sure she'd heard the girl correctly. "Halloween?"

"It's my birthday," Mandy said promptly.

Taylor paused. She'd sworn that she'd asked Mandy when she was getting married.

"You're getting married on your birthday?" Taylor spoke slowly and distinctly. "And your birthday's on Halloween?"

"That's right." A dreamy expression crossed Mandy's face. "I told Tom if we got married on my birthday, then he could be my present."

Taylor smiled weakly, unsure how to respond.

"Pastor Schmidt isn't too keen on it," Mandy continued. "And he nixed my idea of having the reception be a masquerade party."

"Did he?" Taylor tried to keep her expression blank.

"When are you and Nick doing the deed?"

Taylor's eyes widened. She cleared her throat. "Pardon me?"

"Doing the deed." Mandy repeated. "You know, getting married?"

Taylor wondered what the young woman would say if she answered honestly and said never. "Sometime this fall, I think."

"You think?" Mandy frowned. "Don't you know?"

"We'll be firming up the date shortly," Taylor said smoothly. "Now tell me all about this Halloween wedding of yours. It sounds like fun."

"Tom was sure impressed by the car." Taylor cast Nick a sideways glance.

"I know." Nick shook his head. "It's amazing how some guys are so into that stuff."

"What are you saying, some guys?" Taylor said with a smile. "I heard that thirty-two valve, zero-to-sixty stuff coming out of your mouth."

The corners of Nick's lips twitched. "I can talk the talk as well as anyone. But as far as spending seventy-five thousand for a sports car, that's not me."

"Why did you buy it then?"

"My father bought it." Nick's eyes darkened. "Shortly before he died."

He never talked about his father. Every time she'd tried to bring him up, Nick changed the subject. Even though it really wasn't any of her business, she was still curious. His father sounded like a fascinating man.

"Tom told me he and Mandy are getting married on Halloween," Nick said, changing the subject once again. "Said we're invited to the wedding."

Did you tell him we wouldn't be together by

then? Taylor wanted to ask. Instead she forced a smile.

"Did he tell you that Mandy wanted to wear black and have her attendants attired in orange taffeta?"

Nick roared with laughter. "No way."

"It's true. But Pastor Schmidt *nixed* that idea," Taylor said, borrowing Mandy's word. "Now she's wearing white, and the groomsmen will wear black."

"She wanted a black wedding dress?" Nick shook his head in disbelief. "I can't believe she'd even consider it."

"Think who we're talking about here," Taylor said dryly. "Besides, it might have looked elegant."

"Would you ever wear black?"

The offhand question took her by surprise, even though it shouldn't have. After all, he didn't know her, didn't know what her plans for the future were, what type of wedding she wanted. Would they ever see each other after this summer? Would they be friends? Would he come to her wedding? Would she attend his?

"Maybe." Her heart twisted but her lips quirked up in a grin. "Who knows what the future holds? I certainly don't."

By the time Nick dropped Taylor off and got to his house it was after ten.

He quickly changed clothes and pulled out his laptop. Normally he'd be so lost in his work that the hours would go by and he'd scarcely notice. But tonight he couldn't seem to concentrate.

He'd never really thought much about his father's spending habits before. Seventy-five thousand dollars wasn't a large amount of cash, by any means, but the year his father was sick had been a critical time in terms of Lanagan Associates. The company had been in the middle of an expensive conversion project, and money had been tight.

Odd, he'd never considered his father might have had a role in the company's financial troubles.

He shoved the unsettling thought aside and returned his attention to the computer screen. If he didn't keep his mind focused on work, Lanagan Associates would be struggling again, and this time he'd have no one to blame but himself.

# Chapter Eight

Taylor stood in the entryway, her gaze surveying the already crowded ballroom. The party she'd dreaded for weeks lay before her. The past four weeks had been a whirlwind of activity culminating in tonight's event. By evening's end her engagement to Nicholas Lanagan III would be official.

*Engagement.* The last step before marriage, Nana had proclaimed, unaware her happiness unknowingly added to Taylor's guilt.

"Would you relax?" Nick stood at her side, resplendent in his black tux, an easy smile etched on his handsome face. He lightly brushed back a strand of her hair. "It's a party, not an execution."

"Then why do I feel like my head's in a noose and I'm ready to swing?"

"Your body's telling you you need some—" he

grabbed a glass of champagne from a passing waiter and shoved it into her hand "—of this. Give it a try."

"Wouldn't be trying to get me drunk, would you?"

"On one glass?" Nick grinned. "Not hardly."

Taylor glanced at the flute in her hand. Normally she didn't drink. She'd never much liked the taste of alcohol or the funny way it made her feel. Still, this tiny glass couldn't hold more than a half cup of liquid.

She raised the crystal and took a sip. Then another. The bubbles tickled her throat, and the sweet flavor was tasty. Very tasty. Too bad the glass was so small. Upending the flute, she downed the rest in a single gulp. Before her lips were dry, a waiter appeared and replaced it with another.

This time Taylor took it without hesitation. She smiled her thanks and swirled the sparkling wine. "Maybe tonight won't be so bad after all."

Nick quirked one dark brow. "I think we'll make it." A faint light twinkled in the depths of his blue eyes. "One way or another."

She peered over the rim of the champagne glass and surveyed the crowd. *Small get-together, indeed.*

The casual event for twenty she'd envisioned had been replaced by black-tie formal for five hundred. Not quite the same intimate affair Claire and her father had proposed almost a month before. The party had become an event, the social event of the summer, and had taken on a life of its own.

The ball had started rolling when Henry Waters reserved the ballroom of the historic Heritage Hotel in downtown Cedar Ridge. It had picked up speed when he hired a designer out of Denver to do the decorations and an exclusive upscale caterer for the food. It had careened out of control when her grandparents insisted on doing their part by having tropical flowers flown in from Hawaii.

The results lay before her in all their breathtaking splendor. The sweet scent of the tropics invaded every inch of the massive ballroom. Reflections from hundreds of strategically placed candles flickered in the ornate beveled mirrors lining the walls. Tables, topped with linen and edged with lace, surrounded the mahogany dance floor. Sweet melodies reminiscent of a bygone era filled the air.

Waiters in black tie weaved confidently through the milling throng with silver trays balanced aloft, offering crystal glasses filled with golden bubbles. Three bars and double the number of bounteous buffets rimmed the room and offered everything from imported cheeses and breads to prime rib.

Taylor's stomach growled, and she realized she'd been so busy she'd not only skipped breakfast, she'd missed lunch. She stole another glance at one of the buffet tables and promised herself she'd get something to eat soon. Thankfully—even without food—the tension in her neck had vanished with her second glass of the bubbly.

A conscientious waiter commandeered the glass she'd just drained and handed her another. Nick waved away one for himself, his eyes narrowing at the scene before him.

"This is really something."

Taylor turned, surprised at the edge in his voice.

"Henry and your grandparents certainly went all out to put on a nice party."

She forced an enthusiastic smile. "They sure did."

Privately, she could have done without the opulent extravagance. Especially when she knew this engagement would be over before her grandparents got the bill for the flowers. Goodness knows she'd done her best to stop them, but they'd insisted, telling her she needed to realize you only get engaged—and married—once.

*Unless you're Taylor and Nick playing Romeo and Juliet.*

"You look good." Nick's gaze met hers.

Her heart turned over in response, and she said a silent thank-you to her grandmother for insisting she wear something new.

The sleek ivory designer gown with threads of metallic copper fit like it had been created with her in mind. They'd discovered it in an exclusive showroom on Chicago's Michigan Avenue and, though the neckline showed a little too much cleavage, her grandmother had proclaimed it perfect and insisted on buying it. Nana hadn't batted an eye at the exorbitant price.

*Last year I wouldn't have given a second thought to spending that kind of money.*

This year, due to her financial situation, Taylor had planned to make use of one of the many beautiful gowns she already had hanging in her closet. Nana had been appalled, insisting a new dress would be her engagement gift and Chicago would be just the place to find it. Moments later her grandmother had the airline tickets on hold and a suite in Chicago's Palmer House Hotel reserved for the weekend.

Nick had raised an eyebrow when she told him about the shopping trip. Though he didn't say a word, she'd got the distinct impression he didn't approve. *Men.* Who could understand them? And here she thought he'd be happy to have a few days to himself.

His unexpected response confirmed she'd barely scratched the surface when it came to discovering what made her temporary fiancé tick. She'd grown acquainted with the public Nick Lanagan most people knew—the savvy businessman, the charismatic leader, the man who oozed charm when it suited his purposes.

She'd only caught glimpses of the private side of

the man. The Nick who listened respectfully while
her grandfather rambled on about his son's accomplishments. The Nick who'd surprised her and
agreed to attend church services with the family.
The Nick who swung by his secretary's apartment
to check on her after she'd been involved in a minor
fender bender.

"How *is* Miss Dietrich?"

"She'll be back on Monday. The cast came off
yesterday." He studied her face with his enigmatic
gaze for an extra beat. "Why?"

"Just wondering." Taylor gestured across the
room, the large diamond heavy on her finger. "Isn't
that Henry over by the potted palm?"

She pointed in the direction of a portly man looking very much like a penguin under a palm tree.

"That's him, all right." Nick tightened his arm
around her. "Ready?"

She smiled and chugged the last of her champagne. Thankfully the butterflies in her stomach had
flown along with her apprehension. "You bet."

Nick's lips parted in that charming smile she was
coming to know so well, and they slowly made
their way through the throng of well-wishers to the
potted palm and their host.

Despite the earliness of the evening, Henry Waters's glassy-eyed stare told Taylor the man had definitely been enjoying the liquid refreshments. "You
look lovely, my dear."

Her lips twitched. Up close, the man looked even more like a penguin. But she'd never been checked out so thoroughly by any bird. Henry's beady-eyed gaze swept her from head to toe.

"Doesn't Taylor look simply fabulous, my dear?"

Claire sauntered up to her father. She was dressed to kill—or shock—in a red sequined gown that fit like a second skin and left absolutely nothing of her ample curves to the imagination. She afforded Taylor only the briefest of glances.

"Very nice," Claire said. Taylor wondered if she could have been wearing a burlap sack and gotten the same response.

Claire moistened her lips and shifted her gaze to Nick. "Now you, darling, look positively hunky."

Taylor stifled a chuckle, and Nick shot her a warning look.

Henry glanced around and rubbed his hands together. "I'd say anybody who is anybody is right here at our party tonight."

"Speaking of anybody who's anybody—" Claire's voice dropped to a sultry whisper, and she looked like a tigress spotting fresh meat "—look who just walked in. I never thought he'd come. Not all the way from D.C."

Taylor automatically turned toward the front of the ballroom, but the broad shoulders of a tall man in a cowboy hat blocked her view.

Henry didn't bother to look, but his loud, boisterous chuckle attracted the stares of nearby guests. "Claire, darling, half the people here are from Washington. The room's crawling with politicians."

Taylor's grandparents, as well as her parents, had been well acquainted with the Washington social scene, and they'd sent invitations to many of their friends. From the size of the crowd, it appeared most had taken them up on their offer and had flown in for the festivities.

"No more for you." Claire drew an exasperated breath and took the champagne flute her father had just confiscated from a passing waiter and set it on a nearby table. "Daddy, Tony Karelli is on his way over."

A soft gasp escaped Taylor's lips. "Tony? Here?"

Claire arched a brow, and her head swiveled slowly to stare at Taylor. "You know him?"

"Yes. Maybe. I don't know. I guess there could be more than one."

Yeah. Right.

Tony Karelli. They'd met as teenagers. Tony had been smart and incredibly sweet, but a bad case of acne, unfashionable thick-lensed glasses and a tendency toward chubby had made him a social outcast. Taylor had befriended him, and they'd been dubbed Beauty and the Beast by some of their crueler classmates. Over the years, they'd lost touch. Last she'd heard he was in Europe.

Claire's dark eyes glittered. "His father used to be a senator from New York and now is the ambassador to Italy."

"Then it *is* the Tony I knew—"

"I wondered if you'd remember me."

Taylor's heart leaped at the sound of the familiar voice, and she turned toward it. "I'd recognize that East Coast accent anywhere."

"What accent?" The tall broad-shouldered handsome man looked more like a stranger than the Tony she remembered. But the smile hadn't changed, and when he opened his arms for a hug, she wrapped her arms around his neck and let him twirl her around. She buried her face in his neck. Seeing him again brought a deluge of memories.

Almost as if he could read her mind, Tony whispered against her hair. "I'm sorry about your father. I wished I could have been there for you."

She blinked back the unexpected tears that pushed against her lower lids and hugged him tighter. "I know you would have."

"Why, it's little Tony Karelli." Grandpa Bill's amused voice brought Taylor out of her old friend's arms. "See, Kaye, I told you that's who that was."

"Judge Rollins." Tony released her and turned to shake her grandfather's hand. "It's great to see you again, sir. But as you can see I'm not so little anymore.''

"No, you're not. You're all grown-up. How's your father?''

"Busy as ever. He and Mother are still in Italy.''

A warm glow filled Taylor, and she listened to her grandparents quiz Tony about the last few years, barely conscious of Nick's rigid form at her side and Claire's sideways glances. Her grandfather was right, Tony had indeed grown up. The dark hair, as black as Nick's but slightly longer, the brown eyes instead of blue, were just as she remembered, and confirmed this indeed was the Tony of her school days. But beyond that...

A tanned, smooth face gave no hint of the blemishes that had once caused such distress. He'd grown taller—a good six inches if she were guessing—leaving not an ounce of fat on his muscular frame.

"What happened to your glasses?'' Taylor blurted when her grandfather paused for breath.

"Contacts.'' He grinned—something he hadn't done much of when he'd been younger—and she noticed the braces were gone, leaving behind a mouthful of straight white teeth.

Taylor returned his smile, happy that life had been good to her old friend.

"Isn't it funny? You two coming together after all these years at Taylor's engagement party,'' Nana said. "There was a time we thought it would be you and Taylor tying the knot."

Grandpa Bill shot his wife a disapproving glance, and Nana's face grew pink.

"A man would be lucky to have Taylor for a wife." Tony smiled and shook his head. "I can't believe you're getting married."

A warmth crept up the side of Taylor's neck and an awkward silence filled the air. Nick stepped forward and extended his hand.

"I don't believe we've met. I'm Nick Lanagan. Taylor's fiancé." His arm slid proprietarily around her shoulders. "I'm glad you could come and help us celebrate."

Tony shifted from one foot to the other, but his suave facade didn't waver. "Actually, I wasn't on the guest list. I—"

"He's here as my guest, Nick. We're—" Claire rubbed against Tony like a cat "—very good friends."

Taylor's jaw dropped. She shut it with a snap. "Tony?"

Nick's hand tightened around her arm. "Sweetheart, I feel like dancing."

He pressed one hand firmly against her back, and Taylor barely had time to smile her goodbyes before he whisked her onto the dance floor.

The tantalizing smell of his aftershave wrapped

around her and she leaned lightly into him, tilting her face toward his. "Nick. Why did—"

Her last words were smothered by his lips. The kiss was sweet, tender, and it ended as quickly as it began.

"What was that for?" she said, slightly breathless.

"Can't a man kiss his fiancée without having a reason?" he teased. But his gaze slid around the room as if to see if anyone noticed.

Her heart plummeted. Of course it was all an act. For a fleeting moment, she'd forgotten.

Taylor shifted her gaze to the dance floor. Across the room Tony and Claire moved so slowly, they might as well have been standing still. Claire's voluptuous body molded tightly against Tony and they swayed back and forth, never moving beyond the same square foot. Tony's dark head bent over Claire's, and her fingers played with his hair.

"Look at them." She punched Nick in the back.

He turned and watched the two for a moment before shifting his gaze to Taylor. "Jealous?"

"No, of course not." Taylor frowned, and she stole another glance at the non-dancing duo. "It's just that Tony's a good friend."

The faint glimmer of amusement that flickered in Nick's eyes infuriated her.

"Don't you care?"

"Why should I? I'm not interested in the woman.

As far as I'm concerned, if he wants her more power to him.''

A cold knot formed in Taylor's stomach at the thought of that barracuda with her friend. "Nick?''

"If it's about Tony,'' he said, "I wouldn't worry. He's a big boy. I'm sure he can take care of himself.''

How could Nick be so insensitive? He, more than most, knew what Claire was like. She shifted her gaze away from Nick, preferring at that moment to look at anyone—or anything—else. Her gaze stopped abruptly at the sight of Claire kissing Tony.

"I get it now.'' His gaze followed hers. "This is all about him. You still have the hots for your old boyfriend and you're worried he may be taken by the time you're free again.''

"You're crazy.'' Her and Tony? She'd never thought of him as anything but a good friend.

"Stay away from him, Taylor.''

Taylor bristled. "Tony thinks we're engaged. He'd never—''

"Don't bet on it.'' Nick's mouth tightened into a thin hard line. "I saw the way he looked at you.''

"You two having a good time?'' Grandpa Bill and Nana danced to their side.

For a fraction of a second, Nick's face froze.

Taylor swallowed an angry retort and forced her lips to curve upward. "Just wonderful.''

She gazed at Nick and hoped her smile looked

genuine. "I was just telling Nick, engagements are fun but this one can't end too soon for me."

Grandpa Bill looked startled, then chuckled. "Can't wait for that honeymoon, eh?"

"Bill!" Nana said sharply.

The lively twinkle in her grandfather's eye incensed her grandmother, but Grandpa Bill glanced at Taylor and Nick and chuckled once again. "Can't say that I blame you. Can't say I blame you one bit."

# Chapter Nine

Nick pulled out of the hotel's parking garage and activated the CD system. The *Eroica* symphony, the one Taylor always asked to hear, filled the quiet interior.

Nick glanced at his now official fiancée out of the corner of his eye. She'd rested her head against the seat and closed her eyes when she'd first got in, complaining of feeling light-headed, and hadn't looked up since. Thick waves of auburn hair spilled around her shoulders, and her normally rosy complexion seemed more like a soft pale ivory. Never had she looked more beautiful.

Other than their little argument on the dance floor, the evening had gone better than he'd expected. Taylor's performance had been flawless. Lovely and personable, she'd charmed his business associates and even—he swallowed hard—her leading man.

Unfortunately, her old boyfriend's presence had been an all too real reminder that this woman wasn't his. Had she really meant it when she said she couldn't wait for the engagement to end?

He pushed aside the image of her in Tony Karelli's arms and swallowed hard. "I had a great time tonight. You were wonderful."

Taylor's eyes fluttered open. She raised an eyebrow. "Does that mean I get a bonus?"

"Hmm." He pretended to think. "I might be able throw in an extra ten dollars in this week's check."

"Scrooge."

He grinned. "Thanks for the compliment."

"You're not welcome." Despite her words, a tiny smile played at the corners of her lips. "Actually, it *was* a lovely engagement party."

"The kind you've always dreamed of?"

A halfhearted laugh escaped her lips even as a wistful expression dimmed her smile. "I couldn't help but wish my parents were there, though I realize if they were still alive, I wouldn't even be in this fake engagement."

"Sometimes it doesn't feel fake to me." Nick's fingers tightened on the steering wheel.

She lowered her head and turned to the window. "I know. Sometimes it doesn't to me, either."

He leaned back. The tension in his shoulders left in a rush.

Taylor chuckled, a low husky sound. "When Henry climbed on that table..."

Nick laughed. Henry had swayed precariously atop an antique side table, trying to make a toast for almost five minutes, a bottle outstretched in one hand, a glass of champagne in the other. "He would have been okay if Claire hadn't got embarrassed and tried to pull him off."

Taylor giggled. "I thought for a moment, the way she was jerking his arm, she was going to split that dress right up the side."

"Did you see the look she gave Tony when he pulled her away?"

"I don't think anyone could have missed that. Steam was practically pouring out her nose."

"She should have been grateful. Another second or two and Henry would have ended up on the floor, on top of her." Nick pretended to shudder. "That's one scary thought."

"Claire's a beautiful woman," Taylor said matter-of-factly, casting Nick a sideways glance. "Lots of men probably wouldn't mind rolling around on the floor with her."

"They can have her. Now you and I—" he paused and his pulse quickened at the thought "—on that floor, that would be a different story."

"Does it seem a little stuffy in here to you?" Taylor fanned herself with one hand.

Stuffy wasn't a word he would have chosen. Warm? Hot? Intense? Those words better described his torture. He glanced over, hoping to see an answering flame smoldering in her eyes.

He narrowed his gaze. "Are you okay? You don't look so good."

"All of a sudden, I don't feel so good." She pushed a button and lowered the car's window, then rested her head against the door frame. The cool breeze fanned her pale face and lifted her hair like a dark cloud off her shoulders. In the dim light she looked positively green. "Could you pull over for a minute?"

His eyes glanced to the right and left. Concrete blanketed both sides of the well-lit thoroughfare. "Are you going to be sick?"

"No. I don't think so." Taylor shut her eyes. She took a deep breath, and the dark fullness of her lashes brushed against her cheek. "I just need some fresh air. I'll be okay."

Despite her assurance, Nick was not convinced. Cramping the steering wheel, he took a sharp right and headed for a residential area. He eased the car to the nearest curb, slammed it into park and turned off the motor. "Taylor?"

"I'm fine. Really." Her wan smile did little to reassure him. "It was the craziest thing. All of a sudden I got dizzy. And hot. If you're not in any big hurry, I might just walk for a few minutes. Clear my head.''

She brushed the hair from her face with a trembling hand, confirming she wasn't quite as together as she wanted him to believe.

''A walk in the moonlight,'' he quipped, trying to put her at ease. ''How romantic. Mind if I join you?''

Taylor shook her head, then winced at the sudden movement. ''I'd like that.''

By the time he'd gotten out of the car and moved to her door, she already stood outside, swaying slightly in the overgrown grass. But her skin had started to lose its pallor, and pink tinged her lips and cheeks.

''You're looking better.''

Her gaze shifted from the quiet neighborhood to him, and her eyes glittered. ''You're looking pretty good yourself.''

Nick moved a step closer. ''I had a wonderful time tonight.''

''Me, too.'' Her lips curved in a smile. ''Do you remember when I was dancing with Tony and you cut in?''

Nick stiffened, the memory dampening his desire. He remembered, all right. When one dance had turned into three, he'd had enough. Surprisingly, she'd gone into his arms willingly, almost eagerly.

The air had been charged with the same electricity that surrounded them now. "I remember."

"When you put your arms around me—" she smiled at him "—I had the strangest thought."

He quirked one eyebrow.

"What would happen, I said to myself, if I put my arms around your neck—" she took a step forward, resting her hands on his shoulders "—and kissed you. Right there on the dance floor."

Nick cleared the catch in his throat. "Now why would you have wanted to do that?"

Her hand stroked his cheek, and he felt the same nameless stirring deep inside as when he'd kissed her the night she'd agreed to be his fiancée.

"Because, even though I know we don't have a future together, I'm attracted to you."

Her finger traced the firm line of his jaw, and he held his breath. "You've got great-looking eyes, but I'm sure you already know that."

Her hand slid up, her fingers parting his hair into short, narrow rows, "But did anyone tell you that you have really nice hair?"

He took a deep breath and grabbed her hand. "I don't think this is such a good idea."

She murmured in protest and leaned toward him, her eyes focused on his lips. "Kiss me."

"Taylor—"

"C'mon, Nicholas," she whispered, her long

lashes fluttering provocatively against her flushed cheeks. "One little kiss."

She tilted her head just far enough for her lips to meet his. The electricity of the touch short-circuited his good sense. With a groan, he pulled her against him and kissed her. She wound her arms inside his jacket and around his back.

"Hey, what's going on out there?"

Nick stiffened, and his head jerked toward the voice. An elderly man peered from behind the screen door of a house ablaze with lights. A German shepherd barked sharply behind him, battering its body against the wooden frame of the door in an effort to get at them.

*Great.*

"Ignore them." Taylor's husky voice sent the blood coursing through his veins like wildfire.

His breath caught in his throat.

"You've got five seconds to get off my property or I'm calling the cops. This here's a decent neighborhood."

The old man's words hit Nick like a splash of cold water. All of a sudden he saw them as the man had. Car doors open. Standing in the wet grass. He in a tuxedo. She in a formal gown. Wrapped in each other's arms.

*Like two overage high-school kids on prom night with raging hormones and no common sense.*

"We've got to go." Nick gently but firmly

pushed aside Taylor's hands and her protests and settled her into the car, buckling her seat belt before shutting the door.

Back behind the wheel, Nick hit the gas, and the Jag responded, leaving the man and his decent neighborhood far behind.

"How are you doing?"

"I'm okay. Still a little dizzy." Her mouth twisted in a wry grin. "And a lot disappointed."

Nick silently agreed.

They rode the rest of the way to Taylor's house without speaking. The dark interior and smooth ride did little to ease his surging emotions. He assumed Taylor slept. But when he shut off the car, he turned to find a wide-awake gaze focused on him, the green eyes filled with an indefinable emotion.

"Want to come in for coffee?"

He shook his head regretfully. "I don't think that's a good idea."

He waited for her to argue, but she just sighed and released her seat belt.

"You're right." Disappointment clouded her features. "Don't you just hate it?"

"What?"

"Doing the right thing," she said with a heavy sigh. "Sometimes I wish just once I could do what I wanted instead of being so—so *responsible*."

He knew exactly how she felt. When his mother had the business teetering on the edge of bankruptcy, he'd had to be the responsible one. He'd put his life on hold and cleaned up her mess. Yeah, he'd been resentful. And angry. Truth be known, he still was.

"Just once." She sighed again. "I wish I could be reckless instead of responsible."

"If you weren't so *responsible*—" he emphasized the word just as she had "—what would be the first thing you'd do?"

A flush tinged her cheeks. She hesitated, and he could almost see her wondering if she should speak freely. Her candid green eyes met his. "There's no need to discuss it, because it's not going to happen."

"So, what now?"

"I go to my bed. You go home to yours."

"What about Tony?" He didn't know why he said it. All he knew was that he wanted an answer.

"What about him?"

"Are you going back to him once we break up?"

Taylor stared, a frown marring her forehead. "Tony's my friend."

"And Claire used to be my friend."

She shook her head. "I don't think we're defining friend in the same way."

Nick's jaw clenched. He wanted to ask her more about her relationship with Tony but he kept his mouth shut. He had no right to question her. No right at all. In the eyes of the world he might be her fiancé, but her old friend probably knew her better than Nick did. The thought twisted inside him.

They walked to the front door in silence. Nick planned to brush a light kiss across her cheek and say a polite good-night. But she tilted her head at the last second, and the minute his lips met hers, he was lost.

Nick moved his mouth over hers, and in the end it was Taylor who called a halt, backing out of his embrace with a stumble. She stared at him, her breath coming in short puffs, her eyes large and dark with emotion. "I'd better go."

Without giving him a chance to speak, she was gone, the door closing with a thud behind her.

Nick strode to the Jag, and with one flick of the wrist the engine roared to life. He hit the accelerator, and the car jerked from the curb.

What was he thinking? Ever fiber in his body warned him against her. She was a woman with a house filled with priceless antiques, a closet overflowing with designer clothes and debts the size of Pike's Peak. Claire had hit it on the head when she'd said Taylor was just like his mother.

Getting emotionally involved with such a woman made absolutely no sense. But even knowing that, he still couldn't help wanting her.

And that made the least sense of all.

# Chapter Ten

"This might take more time than I first thought." Claire sat forward in her living room chair and leveled at Tony a narrow, glinting gaze. "How long can you stay?"

Tony thought for a moment. The only thing waiting for him in D.C. was the gambling debt his father so unreasonably refused to pay. He had no job, and other than the money Claire had promised him, no source of income. He took a sip of coffee. "As long as you want, sweetheart."

"Good." Her lips curved upward. "We need to plan our strategy." She leaned back against the burgundy leather, and he could almost see her mind go to work.

His gaze lingered on the long expanse of leg visible beneath the pale yellow fabric. When Claire had greeted him at the door dressed in nothing more than a skimpy silk chemise and matching kimono he'd had high hopes. But those were quickly dashed. She'd informed him she'd just hopped out of bed even though it was past eleven. And unfortunately she'd made it clear business was the only thing on her mind.

"She responded to you," Claire said almost to herself.

"I told you she would." Tony spoke with more confidence than he felt. He knew Taylor had been glad to see him. Nonetheless he hadn't missed how her eyes had searched for Nick even while Tony held her firmly in his arms. "She and I have always been close."

"About that." Claire's gaze turned calculating. "How close were you?

"You mean did I ever…?"

"Did you?"

Her hopeful expression said there might be some extra money in it for him if he said yes. Unfortunately if he lied and Claire found out, he'd be dog meat. He'd be better off facing a hundred hungry loan sharks than one angry Claire Waters.

He shook his head and heaved a heartfelt sigh. "I'm afraid not."

"Are you lying to me?" Dark storm clouds formed in her eyes. "Because if you are—"

"Now why would I do that?"

"Because you're old friends." She spit the words out as if they were poison. "Maybe you're trying to protect her."

"I'm telling you the truth, Claire." He took a long sip of coffee. "But you're right, I do want to protect her. That's why I'm here."

She raised a brow.

"Okay, I'm here because I need the money," Tony said. "But I'm here because of her, too. If Nick is the jerk you claim I don't want her to be with him. If I can get her away from him and end up making a few bucks in the bargain, so much the better. Like killing two birds with one stone."

He could see her weighing his words, and under her measuring gaze he felt sixteen again. Awkward. Unsure. The type of guy a woman like this would never look at twice. Tony straightened. He now ran with the beautiful people and got invited to the all the best parties. Any adolescent angst belonged in the past.

"I can't believe the two of you never fooled around." Like a dog with a bone, Claire wouldn't let the subject drop.

"Taylor's saving herself for marriage," Tony said with a shrug.

"You're kidding. She's twenty-six years old."

"I don't know what to tell you." He shifted uncomfortably, once again feeling like he'd been judged and found wanting. "Nothing happened."

"Okay." She moved forward and rested her arms on her knees. "The first step is for the two of you to renew that old friendship. Then you find a way to break them up. It's as simple as that." Claire smiled slyly at him.

Simple? Tony groaned. Even he wasn't foolish enough to believe that.

Taylor stared at the phone, willing it to ring. Willing it to be him. It had been two days since the party, and the only time she'd heard from Nick was when he'd called early on Sunday to say he was skipping church.

Every time the phone rang she hoped she'd hear that rich baritone. But so far she'd fielded two calls from her grandmother and three from telemarketers.

*Please let it ring.*

As if on cue, the shrill ring split the air. She grabbed the phone. "Hello."

"Recovered from the party?"

Taylor recognized Tony's voice immediately. She pushed her disappointment aside. "I think I'm fully recovered," she said. "But then it's been a few days."

"I don't think I'd ever seen you drink so much champagne." A thread of amusement ran through his voice.

"And I can tell you, I won't be doing it again. Ever."

"Headache?" Tony teased.

"The worst. Yesterday, every time I moved, my head throbbed." She never drank. The evening had been so important to her grandparents and so critical to the success of her and Nick's arrangement that she'd tried to calm her fears with alcohol.

*Dear Lord, I'm so sorry.*

She offered up the silent apology. She'd never find the comfort and the strength she needed in a glass of champagne.

"Well, when you feel better, how about we go out? Catch up on old times?"

"I'd like that," Taylor said sincerely. She and Tony had been good friends and they knew a lot of the same people. "Why don't you give me a call in a day or two and we'll set up a time?"

"I'll call you tomorrow."

"I'll hold you to it." She hung up, grateful Tony hadn't asked to set a time now. Normally she would have been more than willing. But if her schedule was booked, she and Nick might not be able to find time to get together.

Her cheeks grew warm just remembering the way she'd acted when they'd last been together. Like a wanton woman. She'd practically thrown herself at him.

What must he be thinking? Was that why he hadn't called?

Taylor straightened and squared her shoulders.

She couldn't change the past, she could only learn from her mistakes and move forward. Today she'd keep herself busy around the house. Tomorrow, if he still hadn't called, she'd find an excuse to call him.

"How was the party?" Erik Nordstrom put his feet up on the glass coffee table, ignoring Nick's censuring look.

Nick tapped his pen against the stack of computer reports piled high in front of him. It was only Tuesday, but Saturday night seemed a million light-years away. "Tell me why you weren't there."

"I already did. My mother was getting married. Again. And she insisted I attend."

Erik's answer barely registered on Nick's short-circuiting brain. Restless and agitated over the news he'd received that morning, Nick pushed back his chair and strode to the side bar. He grabbed his Denver Broncos mug and poured his third cup of the extra-strength coffee Miss Dietrich had brewed.

"I have it on good authority that stuff works just like drain cleaner in your stomach." Erik waved away a cup for himself.

"Forgive me for not listening to someone who relies on trash newspapers at the grocery store checkout lines for information."

"Hey, I'm an inquiring man."

Nick groaned and Erik grinned. His friend's

fondness for the tabloids had been a source of dissension since their freshman year when Erik had convinced him it would be acceptable to list a popular tabloid article as one of their sources on a group research project. Thanks to that lapse in judgment, Nick had pulled the only B in his college career.

"How was the wedding?" Nick asked, more to change the direction of the conversation than out of any real interest. He'd attended the last two with Erik, and they hadn't varied much except for the groom.

"Typical. Same minister, same organist, same singer. If I didn't know better, I'd think she had them all on retainer." He chuckled. "The music was a little different. Remember how the last guy liked the Stones? Well, this one must have been into country because Mother dear walked down the aisle to a steel guitar rendition of 'Here Comes the Bride.'"

Nick choked back a laugh. "Sounds...nice."

"I might be able to get him to play at your wedding." Erik placed a finger to his lips and pretended to think. "If we play our cards right, he might give us a frequent-user discount. What do you think?"

"I think you've been drinking something with a little more kick than this caffeine." Nick gestured with his half-empty cup.

"Nicholas, I'm shocked. You know I never drink

before noon," Erik said. "But seriously, doesn't all this wedding talk sort of get you in the mood?"

Nick smiled, remembering Grandpa Bill's words. "Let's just say you can keep the steel guitar and the ceremony. But the wedding night, now that's different."

"I knew you had the hots for her." A smile of pure satisfaction blanketed Erik's features. "I knew it the moment you told me you'd made her that crazy offer without even thinking it through. It was so impulsive. So unlike you."

Nick shifted uncomfortably. "Like you said, she's a beautiful woman. A man would have to be crazy not to find her attractive."

The image of Tony Karelli's expression as he'd watched them dance flashed in Nick's mind. Karelli was definitely not crazy.

"So the pretend engagement's now official?"

"Announced before five hundred people on Saturday and made the society page in Sunday's edition. You don't get much more official than that." Nick took another sip of coffee.

"Seeing the way you two look at each other would have been enough to convince most people. If I didn't know better, I sure wouldn't have any doubts about whether it's the real thing." Erik shook his head, open admiration in his eyes. "You two deserve Oscars for your performance."

Nick smiled and accepted the compliment. Erik

would be shocked if he knew how little acting was actually involved. Over the past few weeks the once clear line between real and pretend had blurred. Being invited to dinner parties as a couple, golfing with Bill Rollins and being treated as one of the family, even talking with Taylor every day had become part of his life. This morning that fact had been driven home when an employee stopped him in the hall to offer his congratulations and he'd found himself saying, "I'm a lucky man," and meaning it. The closing curtain needed to fall on this charade, and fast. Or Nick Lanagan just might end up in love with his leading lady.

"I think now would be a good time for you to contact Henry's attorneys again. See if you can push things along. Get some of those last few contract issues resolved."

"Merger means end of engagement."

"It'll save me some cash." Nick dropped into his desk chair, picked up the pen and drummed it against the edge of the desk.

"You'll lose your fiancée."

"She's never been mine to lose." He ignored the voice deep inside that insisted Taylor was his girlfriend. His fiancée. *His.*

But she was so wrong for him. And if his heart didn't quite agree, he'd never let it direct his decisions in the past and he wasn't about to start now.

The ringing phone saved him from comment. He motioned for Erik to stay.

"Very well. Put her through." His fingers tightened around the receiver. "Taylor. What's up?"

"I just wanted to let you know that we're golfing Friday afternoon."

"We are?"

"My friend Tiffany called and they needed one more couple for this charity golf scramble. They were desperate and I thought we'd probably be going out anyway...."

"Friday's not good for me." Nick deliberately clipped the words.

"Why not?" she asked.

He steeled himself against the disappointment in her voice and reminded himself it was better this way. "I've got work to do."

"You can't spare one afternoon?"

"I gave you all last weekend," he said brusquely. "This engagement was supposed to give me more free time, not less. Just tell your friend we can't—"

"Don't worry about it. I'll find another partner." Taylor's voice lowered. "Nick, about the other night, I'm a little embarrassed. I never drink and I think the champagne must have affected me more than I thought. If I said or did anything to offend you, I'm really sorry."

"Don't give it a second thought. You didn't do

or say anything I can hold against you.'' The lie slipped easily from Nick's lips, and he smiled when he heard her breathe a sigh of relief.

"Great. I was worried. And about Friday, if Tiffany and I weren't such good friends I would have said no, too. This consulting work is going to take more of my time than I thought.''

"I know they're glad to have your help.''

"It's sort of ironic. You fire me, offer me a job as your fiancée, then hire me as a consultant. What a deal.'' She laughed, and the lilt in her voice that had been there when she'd first called returned. "Hey, Nick, my other line is beeping. I've got to go.''

Nick slowly lowered the receiver to its base and wondered if distancing himself from her really made the best business sense. She certainly hadn't seemed to mind. In fact it was almost as if she didn't care. Of course, he needed to keep in mind she got her five thousand a week whether they saw each other every day or once a month.

"Why aren't you going out with her Friday?'' Erik's voice broke into his thoughts.

"What were you doing? Listening to my conversation?''

"Of course. As much as I could hear, anyway. I should have suggested you put her on speakerphone.'' Erik's teasing expression turned solemn.

"Seriously, Nick, she's supposed to be your fiancée. Why wouldn't you want to be with her?"

*Because I already like her too much.*

"We been together way too much lately." Nick hoped the lie sounded convincing. "Plus I'm not crazy about co-ed golf."

"Still, you need to keep your woman happy."

"That's what the money's for. Believe me, the ink was barely dry on that first check when she cashed it." Nick wondered why he resented paying her when it was all part of the deal.

"Hey, that reminds me of a rumor I heard this morning. Is Taylor going to be doing some consulting work on the Burkhalter project?"

Nick nodded. "She was the team leader on that project before she got downsized. They were going nowhere quick without her."

Erik shook his head. "It really makes no sense why she was let go. Did you ever check on that?"

"Harv from Personnel called me this morning."

"And?"

Nick sighed. "You've got to promise to keep this just between us."

"I'm not sure I like the sound of this." Erik's eyes were serious behind his glasses.

"Apparently there'd been a mistake. The pink slip Taylor received was supposed to go to a Kay, *K-A-Y*, Taylor in the audit department." Nick recognized Erik's shocked expression. He'd worn the same one when he'd heard the news. "Harv apologized all over himself then asked me what I thought we should do."

"And what did you tell him?"

"What could I say? I told him not to mention this to anyone, especially Taylor. I said I'd take care of it. I made it sound like Taylor had a lot on her mind between the wedding and consulting and I didn't want her to feel obligated to go back to work full-time." Nick paused. "He bought it."

"As if this whole fiancée-for-money thing wasn't bad enough." Erik slowly removed his glasses and rubbed the bridge of his nose. "When are you going to tell her?"

"I don't know." Nick set his cup down on the desk slowly and deliberately. "Keep in mind the only reason she'd even considered my offer was because she'd lost her job and needed the money. What's going to happen if she finds out she still has the job?"

"Nick. Listen to me. You have to tell her."

"I don't have to do anything," Nick said, a hard edge to his voice. "I'm paying her a bundle to be my fiancée. Not to mention the money she's earning now as a contract employee. She's not hurting under this arrangement."

The lines of concentration deepened along Erik's brows. "Wake up and smell the lawsuit, Nick. I don't have to remind you she was hesitant enough about agreeing to this engagement. If she finds out you've deceived her—there's no telling what she'll do.''

''Once the merger is complete, I'll give her back her old job. With a raise,'' he added hastily.

Erik leaned back and fit his fingers together. ''You can't believe she'd actually take it.''

''Why not?''

''Because everyone thinks this engagement is real. It's bound to be awkward when it ends. You think for one minute she'll want to come back and work for you like nothing happened?'' Erik shook his head. ''No way.''

''Then I'll give her a great recommendation.''

An incredulous chuckle spurted from Erik's lips. ''I can just see it. Last assignment—fiancée. Job duties—social companion, attractive escort, occasional golf partner.''

Nick clenched his jaw. ''Come off it, Erik. You know what I meant.''

''I've said it before and I'll say it again. You'd better be thinking about keeping that woman happy.'' Erik stood and stretched. ''Happy people are less likely to sue.''

Nick pushed aside his unease and gave a dismissive wave. He'd had his fill of this subject. ''You want to play racquetball Friday night?''

''I thought you were busy with work.''

"We can just play a couple of sets. It helps me relax."

Erik shrugged. "Sure. But if you change your mind and want to do the golfing thing with Taylor..."

"I won't."

As soon as the door closed, Nick leaned back. He knew he should be going with Taylor on Friday. If he had his way, he'd see her every day. But he had to keep reminding himself no good would come out of getting too attached to a woman who was so wrong for him.

# *Chapter Eleven*

Nick returned to his old habit of staying late and coming in early to catch up on the work he'd uncharacteristically let slide the previous week. Thankfully the pile on his desk was dwindling, and he knew he would have the time to golf with Taylor tomorrow. But then, he reminded himself, time had never been the issue.

The door swung open, and Nick groaned. "Miss Dietrich. I thought I told you—" He stopped midsentence and straightened in the chair. "Mother, what a surprise."

Sylvia Lanagan Childs smiled brightly and opened her arms. "What, no kiss?"

He rose, rounded the desk and brushed the obligatory kiss across her cheek. Her skin was soft and smooth, and the faint scent of lavender surrounded her.

"Have a seat." Nick gestured to the chair in front of the desk.

Even though they lived in the same town, it had been almost a year since he'd seen her. He took a minute to study her. Her auburn hair was longer than he remembered, pulled back low at her neck and secured with a tortoiseshell clasp. Although a few strands of gray were visible, her casual linen suit highlighted a still-youthful figure.

Her gaze shifted to meet his. Two lines of worry appeared between her eyes. "You look tired."

"Not tired. Just busy." Nick gestured to the stack of papers sitting before him.

"You're always busy," she said without rancor. "I won't keep you long."

She laid an envelope on the desk. "I'm sorry I missed your party. Charlie and I have been in Switzerland and the invitation must have come when we were gone."

Nick stared. Claire must have gone against his wishes and invited his mother.

"You look surprised." Sylvia's smile wavered. "Don't tell me I wasn't supposed to be invited?"

"Of course you were." He'd thought it would be hard on them both if she came to the party. But he'd failed to take into account how much it would hurt her not to be included. "I didn't know you were out of the country."

Her brow lifted, and he had the feeling she could see right through the lie.

She shoved the envelope across the desktop. "Please accept my congratulations. I hope you and Taylor will be very happy."

Nick stared. She'd given him money. An unreasonable anger rose within him.

"We don't need your money." He spoke more harshly than he'd intended. Didn't she realize everything couldn't be made right with money?

"There's no money in the envelope." Disappointment filled her blue eyes. "Only love and good wishes."

His heart sank lower, and shame filled him.

She rose, her face tight and controlled. "I'll leave you to your work."

"I promise I won't stay but a minute—" Like Erik and then his mother, Taylor burst into Nick's office unannounced. She stopped suddenly, and her eyes widened. "I'm sorry. No one was at the front desk. I didn't realize you had company."

"Miss Dietrich had some errands to run." Nick rose and rounded the desk, brushing a welcoming kiss against her cheek. "Taylor, I'd like you to meet my mother, Sylvia Childs. Mother, my fiancée, Taylor Rollins."

Sylvia stood, and Nick cursed himself for putting the wariness into her gaze.

Thankfully, delight swept Taylor's face and she moved forward immediately to clasp Sylvia's hand, "Mrs. Childs, what a pleasure to finally meet you. I'd hoped to see you at the engagement party. Nick and I were so disappointed you couldn't make it."

*Thank you, God.*

The strain in Sylvia's face eased, and Nick breathed a sigh of relief.

"That's why I stopped by. My husband and I were out of town and I didn't get the invitation until we returned." Sylvia gestured to the cream-colored envelope still unopened on the desktop. "I dropped by with a card. I didn't have time to pick up any—"

"Don't you worry about that," Taylor said, giving his mother a hug. "Your good wishes are all we need."

For a second, Nick swore his mother was going to cry. But when the embrace ended, Sylvia's eyes were dry.

"You're a lucky man, Nick." Sylvia's gaze shifted from Taylor to her son. "You take good care of her."

He swallowed against the sudden lump in his throat. Why did her approval still mean so much? "I will."

"And, Taylor, you make him happy."

Taylor met the older woman's gaze with a directness that surprised even Nick. She was really getting the hang of this acting. "I'll do my best."

"Good." Sylvia hurriedly gathered her purse and blinked rapidly. "Congratulations. I wish you both only the best."

In a matter of seconds she was gone. The door closed softly behind her, and Taylor sank into the chair Sylvia had just vacated. "Your mother seems like a nice woman. I'm glad I got to meet her."

Nick sat in his desk chair, strangely exhausted. His fingers toyed with the card.

"What does it say?"

"I haven't looked at it yet." He pushed it toward her across the slick desktop. "Open it if you want."

It was all the encouragement Taylor needed. "Do you want me to read it out loud?"

Nick shrugged.

"Wishing you love and happiness on your engagement." Taylor held up the card and showed him the outside.

"If you're going to take all day, I've changed my mind. Don't read it."

Taylor ignored him and shifted her attention to the card. "There's no verse inside, just a note from your mother. Maybe you should read it yourself."

He waved a dismissive hand. "Go ahead."

"Okay." Taylor took a breath. "'Dear Nick, Remember what I used to tell you when you were younger, If you always do what you've always done, you'll always get what you always got.'"

Nick groaned and raked his fingers through his hair. He'd heard that a million times when he was growing up. Even when he'd been in college, she'd spouted it to him. When he'd told her he wasn't any good at public speaking, she'd encouraged him to take some speech classes, join the debate team and practice before small groups. She'd said if what he'd been doing hadn't worked, he needed to do something different. She'd been right.

"Go on." Sensing Taylor's curious stare, he shifted his gaze to the ceiling.

She cleared her throat and resumed reading.

"'Make sure that the choices you make, the priorities you set as a couple are the ones that will give you both the true happiness you deserve. Love, Mother.' That's so sweet." Taylor smiled and lowered the paper. "I don't think I've ever heard that saying before."

"It was one of her favorites."

"Does she have any others?" Taylor lifted a brow.

*You love that company more than you love me. More than you love Nick.*

It wasn't a saying as much as a refrain heard over and over. Even now, five years after his father's death, he still railed against the thought.

After all, wasn't it Nick his father had asked to

see while on his deathbed? Hadn't Nick been the
one to hold his father's hand while his life slipped
away? And hadn't Nick been the one he'd entrusted
with his most valuable possession—the company?

Why did the thought suddenly make him sad?

"No," he said, shaking his head. "Anyway,
none that I remember."

Her gaze narrowed, and she studied him thoughtfully but didn't comment. Instead she picked up her
bag and rose. "And you're sure you can't golf tomorrow?"

He used an easy out and gestured to the papers
littering his desk. Work had been his salvation after
his father died. It would have to be again.

# Chapter Twelve

"**I** hope Claire didn't mind you coming with me tonight." Taylor waited while Tony loaded her clubs into his 4x4 Cherokee.

Tony laughed. "You're incredible."

She smiled. "What's so funny?"

"If anyone's going to be upset about you and me being together, it'll be your fiancé."

His arched brow reminded her of Nick, and for a second her heart twisted. Try as she might, she still couldn't understand why he hadn't come with her today.

"You never told me why he bailed on you." Tony's eyes shone with a curious intensity.

"This golf match was last-minute." Taylor forced a shrug. "And Nick had work to do."

"So you're telling me he's not waiting in the wings? You're free for the whole evening?"

"Not free," Taylor pushed thoughts of Nick aside and smiled. "It'll cost you."

Playing along, Tony reached into his pocket and pulled out his wallet. "Okay, how much?"

"There's a Dairy Queen down on Main I've been meaning to check out. Do you have enough for a—"

"Vanilla dip cone with butterscotch?"

"How'd you remember?" She smiled with delight.

"How could I forget? Hanging out at DQ with you was a big deal." Tony reached over and tugged her hair, a familiar gesture from the past. "Tonight, we're going all out. Drinks are on me."

Taylor giggled. The girlish sound made her laugh. "Lime Mr. Mistys?"

"For you, darling, nothing but the best."

She flung her arms around him. "Tony Karelli, you're wonderful."

He reciprocated and wound his arms around her, but instead of a brief squeeze the moment stretched. Was it her imagination or did he seem reluctant to let her go? She finally pulled back, breaking the contact, her gaze searching his face. For what, she wasn't sure. As if sensing her unease, Tony winked, and the warm friendliness in his grin reassured her.

Sitting next to Tony atop one of the weathered

picnic tables in front of the Dairy Queen, she could have been eighteen again. Taylor tossed away the straw and sipped the slush straight from the cup. The bug zapper buzzed overhead and the ice cream turned to liquid faster than she could lick and talk.

Sparkling stars filled the dark sky, and the gentle breeze ruffled Tony's dark hair into little tufts.

Impulsively, Taylor reached over and touched his arm. "I'm so glad we're still friends."

"I've missed you, Taylor," he said quietly. "You were the best part of my life for a long time. Actually, you were my only friend."

Taylor murmured in protest, but Tony just smiled. "It's true. Don't bother to deny it."

"They just couldn't see what a special guy you were." She held up one hand and counted off each finger. "You're loyal, kind, fun to be with—"

"Stop, stop." Tony held up one hand, a flush spreading up his neck. "You're making me sound like a cross between a Boy Scout and Lassie."

Taylor laughed. "All I'm trying to say is you're a great guy. Don't settle for less than you deserve. Promise me that?"

"I promise." His gaze shifted to his drink. "Do you really think your father hoped we'd end up together?"

Taylor took another sip of her Mr. Misty and thought for a moment. She finally nodded. "Probably. He always liked you and your parents."

"He was a great guy. And your mother was the best. They were a perfect couple."

"Yes, they were." Taylor thought of the loving touches and the laughter that had flowed gently between the two. There had never been any doubt their affection ran deep and true. "I always promised myself that would be the kind of love I'd have."

"Do you think you'll have it with Nick?"

"That's an odd question." Taylor forced a laugh. "Of course."

Tony set her drink aside and took her hands in his. "I don't want you to take this wrong. I'm just worried you might have rushed into this engagement. Claire says you two haven't known each other very long. I can understand you being lonely, what with your parents gone and all, but please don't *you* settle for less than you deserve."

She couldn't be cross with him. Still, what if any of this got back to Claire?

"I appreciate your concern. I really do. But you don't need to worry. I love Nick. We're very happy together."

Skepticism shone on Tony's face.

"I'll admit the man's a workaholic, but I'm doing my best to change that."

He reached up and tipped her face to his, his dark eyes solemn. "I want you to promise me if you ever need—"

"If she ever needs anything or anyone, I'll be the one she turns to—right, sweetheart?" Nick dropped down next to her on the picnic table.

Her heart lodged in her throat, and hot guilt spread up her neck. She'd done nothing wrong, so why did she feel like she had?

"Nick. I didn't see you."

His gazed shifted between her and Tony. "I don't doubt it. You two were so *involved.*"

"What brings you to this neighborhood?"

"I just dropped Erik off. We had some business to discuss this evening."

"The scramble was really fun. When you couldn't make it, I called up Tony, and he was able to rearrange his plans. It's too bad you couldn't be there. I think you would have enjoyed it." Taylor stopped and took a deep, calming breath. She detested people who chattered mindlessly.

Nick glanced at Tony, then back at Taylor. His face creased into a sudden smile. "Just being with you, sweetheart, would be enough to make it enjoyable."

Even though she knew he'd slipped into his adoring fiancé role, a comforting warmth invaded her body and it seemed natural to lean her head against his shoulder. His arm wrapped around her. Maybe she'd caught the hang of this acting. Or maybe...

"I'll see her home from here, Karelli."

A muscle twitched in Tony's jaw, but he smiled

at Taylor and nodded to Nick. "I need to get going, anyway. Thanks for inviting me, Taylor. If you ever need a partner—"

"Won't that be a little hard to do from D.C.?" Nick raised a brow.

"Actually, I may be sticking around. At least for the summer. Henry wants me to help him with some project."

"Tony, how wonderful," Taylor said, unable to believe she'd have her friend around for a while longer. "Isn't that great, Nick?"

Nick smiled.

Tony stood and tugged Taylor's hair. "Call me."

"Thanks again for going with me. I had fun." She watched him walk away before turning to Nick. "Maybe while Tony's in Cedar Ridge, you and he can get better acquainted."

Nick stared for a moment then gave her a half smile. "Maybe."

Taylor picked up the slush and took a sip. "I hope so. I think you two have a lot in common."

"Right offhand, I can think of at least one thing," he muttered.

Taylor stared at him, baffled, until she remembered. *Claire.* They'd both been involved with that woman. Taylor frowned. "Nick, about—"

He shook his head and stopped the words and her heart with a simple touch of his fingers against her lips. His solemn gaze swept her face. "I've been doing a lot of thinking these past few days. I've decided as long as the whole world thinks we're engaged, I need to be your escort, your golf partner. After all, I'm supposed to be your fiancé. It's time I started acting like one.''

Acting like one? Dear God, how was she ever going to hold on to her sanity—not to mention her heart—if he really pulled out all the stops? He might be acting, but her response to his words and actions tended to be all too real.

His eyes twinkled, and for a moment she wondered if he knew what kind of thoughts ran through her mind.

Gazing into his deep blue eyes, it was all Taylor could do to resist the urge to venture from the firm solid bank where she'd always stood to a place where she could be over her head in minutes.

Like a shot of whiskey, she downed the last of her slush in a single gulp and jerked upright. Her sudden movement dislodged his hand, and it dropped from her shoulder. All at once she could breathe again.

Until he took the cup from her and set it on the picnic table. His eyes darkened. ''You know what I want.''

''A Mr. Misty of your own?'' she asked weakly.

His cupped hand slid up her arm. ''You're so beautiful you take my breath away.''

Her skin prickled, and a strange kind of electricity filled the air. Taylor forced a laugh and gestured at her shorts and top. "In this? I don't think so."

"It's not what you're wearing." Nick fingered the thin strap of her tank top.

Taylor froze, her heart fluttering wildly.

"Nick, don't."

"Shh, sweetheart." He leaned forward, his hands on her arms. His mouth lowered, and his lips moved over hers. Soft. Gentle. Incredible.

Her heart pounded an erratic rhythm and it took everything she had to make herself pull away. Trying to gain control of her rioting emotions, Taylor shifted her gaze and took a long, steadying breath.

She looked up a moment later to find his gaze on hers. Her mouth went dry. "I..."

"Taylor, I'd like for us to get better acquainted," Nick said softly, curling a loose strand of hair behind her ear. "Let me take you home,"

There was no doubt what he was asking. Taylor paused, thankful she had a ready excuse. "You can't."

"Can't?" His brows drew together.

"I'm spending the night with my grandparents," she said. "There was some kind of chemical spill in my neighborhood this afternoon. The fumes were terrible and the fire department suggested everyone find somewhere else to stay tonight."

She knew she was chattering again but somehow she couldn't stop. A tiny smile lifted the corners of

Nick's lips, and he brushed his knuckles lightly across her cheek. "Call your grandparents and tell them you'll stay at my place."

She shook her head.

"Why not?" A small muscle twitched at the corner of Nick's jaw. "We *are* engaged."

"For the moment." She met his gaze without flinching. "And even if were really engaged, we're not married."

"You can't be serious."

Taylor knew the need that made him push the issue. It gnawed at her, too. But she also knew the difference between right and wrong.

"I'm sorry, Nick." She rested her hand lightly on his forearm. "It's just not going to happen."

"This is incredible." He raked his fingers through his hair.

"Nick, I—"

"It's okay." He jerked to his feet, frustration evident on his face, his fists jammed into his pockets. "It's probably better this way."

He blew out a short harsh breath. His gaze focused intently on the big flashing cone on the roof of the building.

"I know you won't believe this," she said in a soft voice, staring at his rigid features. "But this is hard for me, too."

"Good." Nick let his gaze drop, focusing for a moment on her lips. He forced a smile.

They walked to his car and talked around the tension draped over them like a shroud. The car ride to her grandparents' home was pure torture. Even though he worked hard to keep the conversation light and superficial, beneath the pleasant words an awareness of her fanned a fire that not even the knowledge that nothing was going to happen could douse.

Feeling all of sixteen again, he insisted on walking her to the door. Like a scene from an old movie, he half expected to see the porch light blazing and Gramps peering out the front window. But the night enveloped them in darkness, and the only light shone from the ornate pole at the end of the driveway.

Still, when they reached the steps Nick couldn't help but glance at the front window. The tension in his shoulders eased when he saw the curtains were drawn shut. He turned to Taylor.

Her lips curved in a smile, and she lifted her face expectantly. Nick slipped his fingers into her silky hair and pulled her close. If all he could have was a good-night kiss, he'd make it one she'd remember. One she'd dream about when she slept alone tonight.

He resisted her waiting lips and bent lower, smiling at her sharp intake of air, imparting light feathery kisses where her shirt collar ended and her skin began. She arched her neck, and he planted kisses along her jawline, moving upward, his lips still everywhere but on her mouth.

And then he covered her mouth with his, kissing her with an intensity that shook him to his very core. No one existed but the two of them.

Suddenly the raucous barking of a neighbor dog out for a midnight stroll interrupted them.

The porch light flicked on.

With one supreme effort, Nick pulled back from Taylor's arms. His breath ragged, he slumped against the railing and ran a shaky hand through his hair.

Taylor straightened herself and patted her disheveled hair with a hand as shaky as his. Her eyes glittered in the harsh glare.

It was all he could do not to pull her into his arms again.

"I'd better go in. How do I look?"

*Like someone who's just been thoroughly kissed.*

Nick's gaze lingered. How had this woman managed to get under his skin? "Beautiful. You look beautiful."

Her lips curved in a soft dreamy smile that made him want to kiss her all over again. She reached for the doorknob, then turned and brushed her lips across his. "Sleep well, Nick."

He smiled weakly. Was she kidding? It would be a miracle if he slept at all.

# *Chapter Thirteen*

"What did you think of Pastor's sermon this morning, Nick?" Nana added another dollop of jelly to her toast.

Stopping at the Pioneer Room after church for breakfast had somehow become a regular event, and despite his initial reluctance, Nick found himself looking forward to the Sunday tradition.

He paused and took a sip of coffee, contemplating his response. Technically, the minister was an excellent orator. He interspersed humor into his message, used vocal variation and gestures to full advantage and made good eye contact with his audience. But somehow Nick had the feeling that Nana referred to today's topic, the one that centered around the message of forgiveness. "Excellent sermon."

"What'd you think about it, Taylor?" Nana shifted her attention to her granddaughter.

Taylor sat her glass of milk down. The morning light filtered through the stained glass window and fell softly on her hair, emphasizing the rich red highlights.

"Forgiveness is a hard one." Her brow furrowed in concentration. "I still find myself not always wanting to forgive easily. I think it's because I feel forgiveness sometimes excuses bad behavior."

"I know what you mean." Nana nodded thoughtfully. "That's what I like about Pastor's sermons. They really make you think."

They made you think too much, Nick thought. During the first few weeks he'd attended services with Taylor and her grandparents, he'd been able to tune the minister out. But lately the words had been getting through. It was the oddest thing. No matter how much he tried to concentrate on other things, his thoughts kept straying to the sermon.

And it wasn't enough that he was hit right between the eyes in church, they had to discuss it again over breakfast. It was enough to kill a guy's appetite.

"Nick?"

He glanced up guiltily to find the three of them staring at him expectantly.

Bill smiled knowingly. "I think Nick left us for a while."

"Nana wanted to know if you found it hard to forgive."

Back on the hot seat again, Nick shifted uncomfortably. Hard to forgive? He'd never been a person to hold a grudge. Except when it came to Sylvia.

"Not usually. No." He smiled at Taylor and took a bite of egg. "In fact I've even forgiven your grandfather for beating me at golf Friday."

"You should have seen the look on his face when we tallied up the scores." Bill chuckled. "Taylor, I don't think your fiancé is accustomed to losing to a senior citizen."

"Senior citizen?" Tony Karelli's voice sounded behind Nick. "No way."

"Tony!" Genuine pleasure filled Grandpa Bill's voice. He rose to his feet and clasped the younger man's hand. "And Miss Waters, what a pleasure to see you again."

The eggs Nick had just eaten turned to rocks in his stomach. He pushed back his chair and stood.

"Pull up a couple of chairs. We'd love to have you join us," Bill urged.

"You're so kind," Claire said, almost purring. "And please—" she batted her dark lashes at Bill "—call me Claire."

"Well, Claire." Bill held the chair for the woman. "What brings you and Tony out today? I didn't think I saw you in church."

"Church?" Claire started to laugh, then stopped

and waved a careless hand. "Tony wanted to go on some nature walk at sunrise. He caught me at a weak moment and I agreed."

"When we lived in D.C., Taylor and I used to walk almost every Saturday." Tony smiled at Taylor. "Remember?"

"Of course I remember." Taylor returned his smile. "Every week for almost a year is hard to forget."

Nick narrowed his gaze. He'd known the two had been friends, but he'd never guessed they'd been that close.

"Almost a year." Claire's eyes widened innocently. "Why, after all that talking, I bet you know more about Taylor than Nick does."

"I wouldn't say that." Tony appeared to discount the notion, but the smug look in his eyes told Nick differently.

"People change." Nick took another sip of coffee.

"Do they?" Claire gave a dainty shrug.

Nick glanced at his watch.

"We all change over time," Nana said and offered Nick a smile.

"I know, let's do a little test." Claire flashed a beguiling smile, and Nick's unease increased. He'd seen that smile in the past, and it always spelled trouble. "We'll see how much Tony remembers from those long intimate walks."

"They weren't intimate," Taylor said sharply.

"We were friends, Claire," Tony added.

"Okay, friends. But you knew Taylor pretty well, right?"

Tony nodded.

"Okay, question number one." Claire cast Nick a sideways glance to make sure he was listening. He forced a bored look. "Tony, how many children did Taylor want to have?"

One, Nick thought, maybe two.

"Now keep in mind she may have changed her mind." Tony paused. "But back then she wanted six."

"Six!" The word burst from Nick's lips like a bullet.

Grandpa Bill and Nana smiled. Taylor reddened. Claire laughed.

"I'm afraid he's right," Taylor said with a self-effacing smile. "Growing up as a 'lonely only,' I'd decided long ago that, God willing, I wanted a whole house full of children."

*But six?* Nick could only stare in amazement. Who would ever want that many children?

"So, Taylor, tell me." Claire raised a finger to her lips and studied the other woman. "Where do you think you're going to find a nanny for that many children?"

"I won't have a nanny." Taylor met Claire's disbelieving gaze head-on. "I plan to be a stay-at-home mom. My family will be my priority."

"What do you think of that, Nick?" One dark brow raised, Claire narrowed her eyes. "I seem to remember that at one time you weren't sure if you wanted *any* children."

All eyes shifted to Nick, and he resisted the urge to run a finger inside his suddenly tight collar. He settled for reaching across the table to take Taylor's hand and bring it to his lips. "You forget, Claire. That was before I met Taylor."

"When were you going to spring it on me that you wanted six kids?" Nick's hands clenched the steering wheel, and he kept his gaze focused straight ahead.

"How 'bout after the wedding that's never going to take place?" Taylor said sweetly.

Nick blew a harsh breath, knowing he was being unreasonable but somehow unable to stop. "Who in this day and age wants a half a dozen kids?"

She lifted her gaze, and her green eyes sparkled like emeralds. "I do."

"Well, I don't." He shoved aside an image of little boys with his dark hair and Taylor's green eyes.

"What does it matter?" Taylor said with a shrug. "Pretend you do."

"Pretend? How do you pretend to want six kids?"

"I don't know." Taylor's lips quirked upward, and she leaned back in her seat as if she didn't care that she'd made him look like a child hater in front of her grandparents. "You're a smart guy. I'm sure you'll think of something."

Nick raked his hand through his hair. Clearly he was getting nowhere with this conversation. His foot hit the accelerator, and he pushed the troubling topic to the back of his mind, desperately hoping the subject wouldn't come up again.

The next day, after they'd played a round of golf, Bill Rollins stopped him on the way to the clubhouse and waved the others on. "Six children is a big family, and a big responsibility."

Nick stifled a groan. He ran an honest business. He didn't cheat at golf. Why couldn't he get a break?

"I know Taylor has always been willing to make that commitment, but you have to be willing to make it, too," Bill continued when Nick didn't answer. "Children need both a mother *and* a father around when they're growing up."

Nick knew this was Bill's tactful way of saying he'd noticed how much time Nick spent at the office. But that wouldn't change. Whether he had a wife and children at home or not.

"Are you sure that's what *you* want, Nick?" The older man's face was filled with concern.

Of course it wasn't what he wanted. But how would Bill react to the truth? Probably by worrying that his granddaughter had chosen the wrong man to marry.

*Pretend you do.*

Nick pulled on all those drama classes he'd taken and forced a chuckle. He slapped Bill on the back.

"Call me crazy," he said with what he hoped was a convincing grin, "but I really do."

# Chapter Fourteen

"I had a wonderful time tonight." Taylor inserted the key in her front door and smiled at Nick over her shoulder. "I love to dance."

"It was fun," Nick agreed.

They'd gone to a club in Denver and spent the evening on the dance floor. It was the slow numbers that threatened Nick's resolve to keep things between them light and low-key. With her body pressed against him and her breath warm on his cheek he wanted nothing more than to kiss her senseless and go from there.

"Want to come in for a few minutes? I could make some coffee and..." Taylor paused and a twinkle lit her eyes. "I've got a pint of chocolate chip ice cream we could share."

Nick groaned. He loved ice cream, and she knew

chocolate chip was his favorite. But to go in feeling the way he did right now would be reckless. Foolish.

"Sure. Why not?" He followed her into the dark house, pulling the door shut behind him.

In only minutes the coffee was perking and the small round container of ice cream sat on the counter in front of them.

Taylor reached into the silverware drawer. "One spoon? Or two?"

He knew she was remembering the time they'd stopped at Dairy Queen and shared a hot fudge sundae. And a spoon.

"One," he said.

"One it is." Taylor dropped the other piece of silver into the drawer and turned, dipping the lone spoon into the soft creamy treat. She took a bite, and her eyes half closed as she savored the taste. "Oh, wow. This is so good."

"I bet it is." He couldn't keep from smiling. Taylor was the first woman he'd known who liked ice cream as much as he did.

She held out the spoon and he hesitated, not wanting to end her pleasure.

"Sweetheart, I can get you another spoon," she said. "It's no problem, really."

He liked the way she said "sweetheart." She'd started calling him that more frequently lately, even when they were alone.

"Now why wouldn't I want to share with you?"

"I don't know." She shrugged. "I could be coming down with a cold. You could end up stuck in bed for a week."

"I'm used to taking chances," he said finally. He moved closer and took the spoon from her hand, setting it on the counter.

"Don't you want some?" Teasing filled her gaze. "I can't eat it all."

"I want something," Nick said, slipping his arm around Taylor and pulling her to him. "But it's not ice cream."

Soft and warm, she was next to him and all he could think was this was the way it was meant to be. He gently touched her face.

Her arms wrapped around his neck. Nick stopped talking and lost himself in their kiss. Not sure of what he'd planned to say, he was past the point of caring.

His resolve to keep his distance vanished in the moment. Suddenly he couldn't get close enough.

He wasn't even aware they were moving until Taylor's back hit the edge of the counter. Taylor seemed to have difficulty breathing and a rush of pink stained her cheeks.

"Let's go upstairs." His voice came out husky and shakier than he would have liked.

Taylor's gaze rose. "Upstairs?"

"To the bedroom." All the reasons he should

back off seemed inconsequential. He would make her his. Tonight he would make love to her until all doubts were swept away.

"Nick."

Her sultry voice sent shivers of anticipation coursing through his veins.

"Yes, my love?" Lightly he fingered a loose strand of hair on her cheek.

She drew a ragged breath and exhaled slowly. "If I led you on, I'm sorry…"

He stared, disbelieving. She'd wanted this as much as he had, he was sure of it. "What are you saying?"

She sidestepped his embrace and gestured to the door. "I think it's time you leave."

Too caught up in his feelings, he scarcely noticed the regret in her eyes or heard her words as she ushered him out the door. "Before we both do something we'll regret."

"I'll have a tall caramel macchiato, please." Taylor stood at the coffee shop counter. She'd have to settle for a dinner of only salad to offset the calories, but for once she didn't care.

"Whipped cream?" The young woman behind the counter poised the can above the drink.

"Please." Taylor reached into her billfold and pulled out a five-dollar bill.

"Taylor." A feminine voice sounded from behind her, and she turned.

"Mrs. Childs." Taylor smiled warmly. "I didn't expect to see you here."

"I was out shopping and decided to take a break. The vanilla latte was calling my name." Nick's mother's smile wavered. "I put my bags at the table over there. Would you care to join me?"

Taylor thought quickly. The few errands she had left could wait. "I'd love to."

They chatted while Sylvia got the latte that was calling her name, then they headed to the table by the window.

The shop looked out onto the town square. Several years before, the city planners had taken a good hard look at the blight and decay downtown and embarked on a massive revitalization project.

Most shoppers still frequented the mall at the edge of town, but the area known simply as Town Square had managed to achieve its own loyal following. The old brick buildings from the turn of the century had been renovated without losing the charm from that earlier era. Merchants had discovered that there were women and men willing to pay more for their high-end merchandise.

Taylor loved to browse in the exclusive shops, even though she could no longer afford the prices.

"Looks like you did some damage." Taylor gestured to the sacks Sylvia had propped up between them on the ledge lining the front windows.

"It's not as bad as it looks." Sylvia took a sip of her latte. "Charlie desperately needed some new clothes, and McMurrays was having a big sale."

"Really?" Taylor raised a brow. Grandpa Bill's birthday was coming up, and he bought all his clothes at McMurrays. Although small, the shop always seemed to have a good selection of the finest menswear. And the service was superb. "I might have to stop over and see what they have."

"Georgine's is having a sale, too." Sylvia's gaze settled on Taylor's stretched silk boatneck sweater, obviously recognizing it as coming from the trendy boutique.

Taylor smiled. Little did Nick's mother know, the garment she'd coupled with a pair of linen slacks was three years old. "I love that store."

"I was just on my way over there. Would you care to join me?"

Taylor's purse was empty, and for the past year she'd used her credit card for emergencies only. Still, what would it hurt to browse?

"Sure, why not? It never hurts to look."

"Or buy." Nick's mother laughed.

"I'll drink to that." Taylor held her caramel macchiato up in a toast.

If the two women weren't laughing so hard they might have noticed the attractive brunette standing on the sidewalk with a grin on her full red lips that would do a Cheshire cat proud.

"Daddy." Claire pushed open the door to her father's office, ignoring his secretary's frantic wave. She stopped in the doorway, her smile widening at the sight. This was going to work out perfectly.

The two looked up at the same time. Her father's lips curved in a welcoming smile, but after giving her a perfunctory nod, Nick returned his gaze almost immediately to the papers spread out on the worktable.

"Henry, about—"

"Nick, let's take a break. Helen." Henry bellowed to his secretary. "Bring us some iced tea."

Claire moved to her father's side and gave him a peck on the cheek. She slanted Nick a sideways glance.

The man was too handsome for his own good. And much too arrogant. He deserved to be taken down a peg or two.

"Daddy, I saw Jack Corrigan downtown this morning and he said to tell you hello."

Nick's jaw tightened. Claire smiled with satisfaction.

"How's he doing?"

"Good." Claire pulled up a chair and sat down across from Nick. She wanted to be able to see his expression when she twisted the knife. "He's considering an offer from some west coast firm."

"An offer?" Her father straightened. "What kind of offer?"

"It's a merger thing." Claire shook her head and pasted a sad expression on her face. "Poor Jack. I think it really hurt him when you didn't choose his firm. After all, you two have been friends for years."

"Jack understood," Henry blustered, clearly uncomfortable. "It was business."

A muscle jumped in Nick's jaw. Claire's heart quickened.

"But I told him not to rush into anything." She widened her eyes innocently. "A deal's not done until the papers are signed."

She could almost see the anger bubble to the surface of Nick's carefully controlled features. Excitement raced up Claire's spine. Now came the real fun.

"By the way." She turned her gaze to Nick. "I saw your fiancée today."

Confusion clouded his gaze. Her adrenaline surged. She'd caught him off guard.

"You did? Where?"

"Downtown." Claire smiled brightly. "Shopping with your mother. Why between them they must have had a dozen sacks. Isn't it nice, Daddy?"

"Nice?" Henry frowned.

"Yes, nice." She shifted her gaze to Nick. Their eyes met. Her words may have been directed to her father, but they were strictly for the other man's benefit. "Nick really did get himself a woman just like his mother."

*Just like his mother.*

Nick's glove slammed into the punching bag.

If Taylor wanted to squander the whole five thousand dollars he'd paid her this week on clothes, he didn't care.

He narrowed his gaze and hit the bag again. Hard.

If Taylor didn't want him, he didn't care.

Like a bullet fired from a gun, his hand shot out, striking the leather. The force of the impact sent the bag swinging wildly.

He steadied the bag and took a deep breath, wiping the sweat from his forehead with the back of his gloved hand.

"Hey, Nick." A guy he vaguely recalled from a golf tournament last year yelled across the room. "Leave a little leather on that bag, will you?"

Nick acknowledged the greeting with a grunt and a nod then turned his attention back to the bag.

Right. Left. Right. Left.

Now he had the rhythm. After five minutes the tension in his shoulders began to ease. After ten, the unreasonable anger that had led him to cancel his afternoon appointments vanished. After twenty, he was exhausted, and the only emotion remaining was disappointment.

With all the women in the world, why did he have to go and fall in love with one just like his mother?

Fall in love? He sank down on a nearby bench, his mind reeling. He couldn't be in love with her. After all, this was all an act. Wasn't it?

# Chapter Fifteen

"Nick, about the other night..." Taylor paused, then tried again. "I hope you don't think I'm making a mountain out of a—aargh!" Frustrated, Taylor whirled and plopped down on the bed. If it sounded stupid in the privacy of her grandparents' guest room, how would it sound when she tried to say it in person?

He'd wanted to spend the night with her. That had come through loud and clear. And she'd surprised him when she'd said no. She knew lots of women who would have jumped at the chance. Claire Waters, for one. She shoved the unpleasant thought aside.

Nick was a handsome man. She enjoyed his company. They laughed at the same jokes and shared a love of chocolate chip ice cream and golf. And she couldn't deny that underneath their friendship a current of desire surged like a raging river. She could control the lust. What made it harder to stay the course was the love.

The notion that she was falling in love with Nick had nagged at the edge of her thoughts for days. Taylor sighed, realizing she'd done just what she'd sworn she'd never do—she'd fallen in love with her leading man. That's why this role had become so easy to play. She didn't have to *act* like a woman in love because she *was* a woman in love.

But did he feel the same? That was the question that had kept her up half the night. Somewhere around three she'd dozed into an uneasy slumber.

Taylor grabbed her robe and headed down the stairs. First she'd have a good breakfast. Then, on a full stomach, she'd think about what she was going to do about Nick.

"Taylor. What a surprise." A sinking feeling gripped Nick's gut, but he smiled past his unease. Her showing up unexpectedly at his office was not a good sign. He motioned for her to take a seat.

"Good morning." She flashed him a too-bright smile.

Although she was as beautiful as ever, with her hair shiny and soft and hanging in loose waves to her shoulders and her eyes that startling shade of green he liked so much, the lines of fatigue on her face were evident.

He could empathize. In the past few days his emotions had been on a roller coaster ride, and the trip had played havoc with his sleep.

He'd wanted her so badly he ached. But not just physically. Having Tony hanging around had sent a shiver of fear racing down his spine. In his haste he'd been reckless. He'd moved too fast. But he couldn't lose her. He couldn't lose what they had.

There was something about Taylor that made him feel warm inside, that made him think about sitting in front of a fire on a cold winter day with a dog at his feet and her at his side. Warm inside? Nick gave a strangled groan. He'd been burning with a different kind of fire last night.

"Did you say something?" She looked at him expectantly.

"Before you start…I want you to know I'm sorry about last night." Nick raked his fingers through his hair. Apologizing like this was awkward. He should have gone to her immediately this morning and cleared the air. Not made her come to him. After all, what would it have taken? A few minutes out of his day? Instead he'd done what he always did and had gone to the office and concentrated on his business.

*If you always do what you've always done…*

Nick shoved the disturbing thought aside and returned his attention to Taylor.

She shifted uncomfortably as if the soft leather of his office chair had suddenly turned hard. "We need to talk."

Were there four more dreaded words in the English language? He flashed her a grin. "I thought that's what we were doing now."

Her lips smiled but her eyes remained somber. "Do you want to start or should I?"

There was that serious tone again. Did he really want to hear what she had to say? Unable to sit still for a moment longer, Nick got up and paced. "Go ahead."

"I'd feel better if you sat down." She gestured to the chair next to her, and he noticed her hand trembled slightly.

She looked so stressed Nick didn't have the heart to say no. He grabbed the chair and turned it toward her before he sat down.

A sudden chill hung in the air, and he wanted nothing more than to take her hand and tell her that together there was nothing they couldn't work out. Instead he flicked away an imaginary piece of lint and remained silent.

"Okay." The word came out on a long exhale. She clasped her hands in her lap and shut her eyes for the briefest time. For a second he thought she might be praying, but the moment passed too quickly for that.

Nick leaned back and rested his elbows on the arms of the chair, hoping he looked relaxed and unconcerned.

"My faith has been a part of me for as long as I can remember." Her gaze sought his, and he gave her an encouraging nod.

"I believe in God's word and I try to live a God-pleasing life." Taylor brushed a strand of hair behind her ear with a trembling finger.

Nick stifled a groan. He held up one hand. "No need to say more. I get the point."

"I don't think you do," Taylor said softly. "I'm not just talking about you wanting more from me. I'm just as guilty of wanting more, too."

"Then why...?"

"There's more to this issue than just the desire." Her voice was calm and matter-of-fact, but a telltale flush rose up her cheeks. "I don't want to just sleep with or have sex with someone, I want to make love. And," she added, "I want that person to be my husband. I want it to be something special, just between the two of us for the rest of our life. Not just with someone I'm hired out to for the summer."

"Is that all I am to you?" Pain made Nick speak more harshly than he'd intended. "Your employer?"

A troubled look crossed her face, but her expression remained determined. She answered his question with one of her own. "Tell me, Nick, what's the most important thing in your life?"

He didn't even stop to think. His response was automatic. "This company. Making it stronger so it's the biggest and the best."

"That's what I thought you'd say." A sad half smile creased her lips.

For one crazy instant he was tempted to take her in his arms and kiss that sadness away. Tempted to tell her that *she* was the most important thing in his life. But he held back as he always did when he got a wild impulse, and the urge passed. "What does that have do with anything, anyway?"

"It shows how far apart we are on everything that matters."

"We're not that far apart." Nick leaned forward and used his most persuasive tone. How could she act as if what had existed between the two of them these past months meant nothing? "We get along great. You like to golf. I like to golf—"

"This isn't about golf. Or about chocolate chip ice cream. It's about who we are in here." Her hand rose in a fist over her heart.

"I guess I didn't think I was that bad of a guy," Nick said stiffly.

"You're not." Taylor drew a shaky breath. "I'm just saying that our priorities are worlds apart. What we want out of life is different and because of that there can never be anything more between us.''

Her large emerald eyes glistened but he paid no attention. He clenched his jaw and drew a ragged breath.

''What's most important in my life is God and my family,'' Taylor said. ''I don't put my job above everything else.''

''That's easy for you to say,'' Nick said. ''You don't have five hundred people depending on you for a paycheck every month.''

''You're right, I don't,'' she said softly. ''But I truly believe that all things work together for the good of those who love God and put *Him* first in their lives. And, as far as business is concerned, what does it all matter if we don't come home at night to someone who loves us?''

''I suppose this is where the pitter-patter of twelve little feet come in?'' Nick said sarcastically.

''That's right.'' Her gaze met his. ''When your father was dying, what mattered in that instant? Having his wife and son at his side? Knowing a loving Saviour was waiting for him with open arms? Or how many people he employed?''

His father's last breath? The memory was too vivid to ever be forgotten. ''Take care of the company,'' his father had whispered to him. There were no loving last words for his wife sitting at the bedside. Or for his son.

"This is getting way too serious." Nick forced a light tone and an easy smile to his lips. "Why don't we just agree to disagree?"

"Agree to disagree?" Taylor's brow furrowed in a frown.

"Yeah," he said with a casual shrug that belied the pain in his heart. "Like you said, we're so far apart on what we believe, why even discuss it?"

"And what about us?"

"What us?" he said, proud he could sound so offhand while his heart was breaking. "You were the one that said there could never be anything between us."

"I was hoping I was wrong," she said softly. "That you wanted more from me than just a good time."

He steeled himself against the hurt in her eyes and shrugged. "You are a beautiful woman."

Taylor flinched as if he'd slapped her. She grabbed her bag and jerked to her feet, her eyes flashing emerald sparks. "I wish I'd never agreed to all this."

"Well, I wish I'd never asked." He felt like a recalcitrant child talking back, trying to one-up her, but he couldn't seem to stop. "I should have given you your old job back the second I realized it was all a mistake."

"My old job?" Taylor froze in the doorway. "What are you talking about?"

Nick's stomach clenched. He cursed his impulsiveness. This wasn't how he'd wanted to tell her. "I didn't find out until recently that there had been a mistake, that the pink slip had actually been meant for Kay Taylor in the audit department, not you. Funny, huh?"

Taylor's lips pressed together, and there was no amusement in her steely-eyed gaze. "Why didn't you tell me when you first found out?"

*Because I was afraid to lose you.*

"What would have been the point?" He kept all expression from his voice.

"I thought I knew you," she said slowly. "I guess I never did."

"I guess not."

Her gaze searched his face, and as she turned he could see her bottom lip start to tremble.

He could have stopped her. There was still time. But it had never been his style to beg.

*You want me as much as I want you.* He wanted to yell the words, to have the last say, but what would that have proved? Her response in his arms the other night told him she wanted him. Her words today told him she wouldn't have him. The door closed on his silence.

Hot anger surged, and suddenly Nick had to get away. From the picture on his desk of his father holding up a trophy he'd been awarded for some business achievement. From Taylor's perfume lingering in the air making his chest constrict with each breath. From his own thoughts.

With no real purpose in mind, Nick drove downtown and parked. He walked the Town Square, glancing in the windows of stores with no real interest in going inside. Even on a good day he hated to shop. And although the sky was bright and sunny, today was definitely not turning out to be a good day.

The huge shade trees blanketing the center of the square beckoned to him, promising a welcome respite from the scorching midday sun.

He sent up a silent plea for some solitude as he headed down one of the concrete paths through the parklike area. His prayer wasn't answered. The place teemed with mothers and their children, older people resting on strategically placed benches and shoppers taking a shortcut across the square.

When the second stroller clipped his ankle Nick sought refuge on a nearby bench. He pulled out his electronic scheduler but quickly placed it back in his pocket. What did it matter what his next week's calendar held when the woman he loved wouldn't have him?

"Is there room for two on that bench?"

Nick lifted his gaze. Dressed in a yellow sundress that accentuated her deep rich tan, Claire stood with a shopping bag in one hand and her purse in the other. Under his scrutiny, she shifted from one foot to the other, an uncharacteristic blush stealing its way up her neck.

There should have been only one answer, a firm no. But it was that hint of uncertainty on her face that caused Nick to hesitate. That and the fact that, unlike Taylor, here was a woman who wanted him.

"Of course there's room." He shoved aside the little voice that said he was being disloyal to Taylor. After all, how could you cheat on someone who was only in it for the money?

Claire's wary look eased into a big smile. "It's a beautiful day, isn't it?"

Nick shrugged. "I guess."

"I'm surprised Taylor isn't here with you."

"She has her life. I have mine." Disappointment made him speak more frankly than he'd intended.

"I've missed you, Nick," Claire said softly. "We used to have a lot of fun together."

If she'd said something negative about Taylor or his engagement, Nick would have been on guard, but her simple statement touched that part of his heart that had been wounded by Taylor's words.

"We did." Nick nodded, conveniently forgetting that those times were few and far between. "But now you've got Tony to show you a good time."

"He'd rather be with Taylor," Claire said.

The look in her eyes told him she was telling the truth. His heart clenched. Nick forced what he hoped was a disinterested smile. "Is that so?"

"It doesn't matter." Claire shrugged. "I don't want someone who doesn't want me."

"Me, either." He thought of Taylor and the way she'd so callously dismissed him from her life.

"Anyway..." Claire leaned toward him. "I'd much rather be with you."

With one hand Nick pushed Claire's hair from her face, caressing her cheek with a finger.

Claire put her arms around his neck and brushed his lips with hers.

"What's going on here!"

The angry voice sounded from the sidewalk. Nick immediately released his hold on Claire and slowly looked up, right into the horrified eyes of Bill Rollins.

"Bill!"

"What the..." Taylor's grandfather took a deep breath and visibly reined in his temper. "Will someone tell me what's going on here?"

The older man's words were sharp and curt, but it was the disappointment in his eyes that cut Nick like a knife.

"What does it look like?" Claire smirked.

Nick resisted the urge to throttle her. How could he have let things get so out of hand? "Claire, Bill and I need to talk. Alone."

She opened her mouth, but he quelled her protest with a glance. "Please."

There was no softness in his tone and no question that he expected her to comply.

With all the drama of a born actress, Claire rose from the bench, making a great show of straightening her dress. "Nick, sweetheart, I'll be home after six. Call me."

Nick gritted his teeth and waited until she was out of sight before he spoke. "I know what this must look like—"

"It looks like you're cheating on my granddaughter," Bill said with a level gaze. "Is that what you're doing? Cheating on Taylor?"

Nick, who'd always prided himself on controlling his emotions no matter how stressful the situation, couldn't stop a hot guilty flush from creeping up his neck.

"Taylor and I have been having some problems," he said, forcing himself to meet the older man's gaze.

"And you think turning to another woman will solve them?" Clearly incredulous, Bill could only stare.

Nick swallowed hard. He hadn't been fair to himself. Or to Taylor. Or to Claire. "It was stupid."

"You bet it was stupid," Bill said forcefully. The man's gaze turned sharp and assessing. "I'm going to ask you a question and I want you to be honest with me. Do you love my granddaughter?"

Did he love Taylor? Nick thought for a long moment and searched his heart, pushing aside the angry words they'd exchanged this morning. "I do. Very much."

Bill heaved a relieved sigh. "Then go to her. Work out whatever problems you're having *together*. Pray to the Almighty for guidance. He's helped Kaye and me through many a rough time. He can do the same for you. You just need to ask."

Nick sighed. If only it could be that simple.

# Chapter Sixteen

"Taylor, it *is* you." A thread of pleasure ran through Nana's voice. "I didn't expect to see you again so soon."

Taylor stiffened over the dresser drawer and didn't turn around. She hurriedly brushed the tears from her cheeks with the tips of her fingers. Certain no one would be home, she'd stopped at her grandparents' house to pick up some clothes she'd forgotten when she'd spent the night. "I thought you'd be at bridge."

"So did I." Her grandmother laughed. "I got all the way over to Betty's only to find that Margie and Eleanor have the flu. So we're skipping this week."

"That's too bad," Taylor mumbled.

A gentle hand settled on her shoulder. "Honey, is something wrong?"

Wrong? At this moment Taylor wondered if there was anything right with her life.

"What could be wrong?" Her attempt at a light laugh ended as a choked sob.

Nana turned her around, and although Taylor kept her gaze lowered she knew her grandmother would have to be blind not to see her swollen lids and blotchy face.

"Nick and I had a fight." Despite her best efforts, Taylor's voice quivered.

"Every couple has their disagreements," Nana said softly. "And it's not all bad."

"How can you say that?" Taylor lifted her gaze. "What's good about fighting with someone you love?"

The last word ended in a wail, and Taylor knew what she'd tried to deny for so long was true. Despite everything, she loved Nick.

"Let's sit down." Nana maneuvered her to the bed, and they sat next to each other on the edge. "Do you want to tell me what happened?"

Taylor shook her head. Tell her grandmother Nick didn't love her? That he didn't want to marry her but he'd sure wanted to spend the night with her? That he knew she'd been fired in error but for his own sake he'd withheld that information?

Nana remained silent, waiting for an explanation Taylor didn't want to give.

"We...we had words," Taylor finally managed to say. "I think it's over. He's not the man I thought he was."

"It hurts, doesn't it?"

That horrible ache returned, and all Taylor could do was nod. Whatever she'd expected, it wasn't this. Nana didn't even try to defend Nick or tell Taylor she could be wrong.

"I don't know who's right or who's wrong in this situation," Nana said, almost as if she could read Taylor's thoughts. "But I have lived long enough to know that at one time or another those we love will disappoint us."

"But the things he said to me—"

"Taylor." Her grandmother's voice was firm. "Stop and think about what I just said. *At one time or another those we love will disappoint us.*" Nana repeated the words slowly, emphasizing each one.

"So what am I supposed to do? Overlook it?" Strident and shaky, Taylor's voice rose. "Go on as if nothing happened?"

"No." Nana's troubled eyes met hers. "I'm saying you leave your pride at the door and search your heart. Turn it over to God. Ask Him for guidance. He knows better than you and I what is best."

"I don't know..." Taylor drew a ragged breath. "Maybe you and Nick aren't meant to be together," Nana said slowly, her voice filled with regret and sadness.

Two months ago, if Taylor could have envisioned a perfect end to her temporary engagement, it would have been this, her grandmother agreeing with her that it was time for the relationship to end. But along the way, what Taylor saw as the perfect ending had changed.

"Do you believe that?" Taylor could hardly force the question past her lips.

"I don't know him as well as you do." Nana laid a hand over Taylor's. "But what I see I like."

"I thought I did, too," Taylor said. "After what he said this morning, I'm not so sure."

"Talk is cheap," Nana said. "Sometimes we say things because we're hurting or to cover up our true feelings. Or maybe he really is a mean person. But I can't believe you'd have agreed to marry someone like that."

"Nick's a good guy." The words slipped out automatically.

"Then don't make any quick decisions." Nana slipped her arm around Taylor's shoulders and gave a squeeze. "Mull it over, pray about it. Don't throw it all away unless you're sure."

Her grandmother's eyes were filled with love and caring. Taylor had no doubt both Nana and Grandpa Bill would support any decision she made. Her heart warmed, and she breathed a prayer of thanks.

She'd been truly blessed to have been born into this family. "I love you, Nana."

"I love you, too, honey."

She leaned her head against her grandmother's, and Nana's arms closed around her.

"It's going to be okay, isn't it?" Her words were muffled against Nana's chest.

"It's going to be fine," Nana said firmly. "God will see to that."


Nick waited until Bill was out of sight before he finally rose from the bench and headed toward his car. His cell phone rang just as he slid behind the wheel. "Lanagan."

"Nick, it's Erik. I've got great news." Bubbling with excitement, his friend rattled on without waiting for Nick to speak. "We've come to a resolution on that final snag in the merger negotiations, and I think we're going to be ready to sign before you can say, 'How much money will we make on this deal?'"

It was what Nick had been hoping for, dreaming of, for the past four years. Why did it suddenly not seem so important?

*If you always do what you've always done, you'll always get what you always got.*

Well, he'd done what he'd always done and he'd gotten what he wanted.

*But you lost Taylor.* A band tightened around his chest.

"Nick? Are you there?"

"I'm here." Nick rubbed a weary hand across his forehead.

"Did you hear what I said?"

"I did." Nick forced some enthusiasm into his voice. After all, it wasn't Erik's fault he didn't feel like celebrating. "It's great news. Good work."

"I'll let you know when the papers are ready," Erik said. "We need to get these signed as soon as possible. Henry's too much of a powder keg. I won't feel good until his signature is on that contract."

An image of Claire striking a match to that powder keg flashed in his mind. "Call me when they're ready."

"Will do," Erik said. "I'll be in the office for another couple of hours if you want to run through these changes."

Nick thought for a moment. Even though he'd already approved the changes, he should review the final document. But he couldn't seem to summon up any enthusiasm. Not with so much else weighing on his mind.

"I'm not sure if I'll be back in today or not. Go ahead and have them typed up," Nick said. "Let me know when the final copy is ready."

"No problem," Erik said. "And, Nick..."

"Yeah?"

"Tell Taylor hello for me."

Nick clicked off the phone without answering and fired up the engine. He pulled away from the curb, despair seeping into every pore of his being.

*Dear God, where do I go from here?*

He drove automatically, not sure where he was headed. But no matter how far he drove, his thoughts kept returning to Taylor.

"Get the junker off the road!" a voice bellowed.

Nick's gaze jerked ahead. Traffic had slowed to a stop, but he'd barely noticed. Now he saw the reason. An all-too-familiar yellow vehicle with its hood up blocked the right lane. Standing to the car's side, looking young and forlorn, was Tom from their premarital counseling class.

The guy in the car in front of Nick laid on his horn. A woman in a small foreign car added her high-pitched beep to the fray.

Tom raked his fingers through his hair and stuck his head beneath the hood.

Without thinking, Nick put his car in park, opened the door and headed toward the Gremlin, weaving his way through the row of cars.

"Put the hood down," he said when he got close enough for Tom to hear him over the honking horns. "I'll help you push it off to the side."

Relief flooded the boy's face. He didn't argue. The hood slammed shut.

"Roll down the window and get in." Nick calculated the distance to a small shoulder area up ahead. "You steer and I'll push."

Tom slid behind the wheel, and Nick forcefully leaned against the vehicle. The car didn't budge. The boy still had it in gear! He stifled a curse.

"Put it in neutral," he ordered, and pushed again. Slowly the Gremlin crept forward. "Cramp the wheel to the right."

Nick put his shoulder against the car, and with one final effort, the car rolled out of the traffic lane and onto the shoulder.

"Grab your keys and come with me." With his eyes focused on the Jag, Nick didn't even look back to make sure Tom followed.

The boy slid into the passenger seat just as Nick shifted into first gear and took off.

"What happened?" Nick slanted Tom a sideways glance. "Out of gas?"

"I wish," Tom said with a heavy sigh. "It just died."

"Do you want to call a tow truck?" Nick gestured to his cell phone. "Or I can drop you off somewhere?"

Tom thought for a moment. "Mandy's at the church for some meeting. She has a car. If it wouldn't be too far out of your way..."

"No problem," Nick said. Spending time with

Tom might be just what he needed to help keep his mind off his own problems.

Unfortunately the trip to the church only took a few minutes.

"I think that's her mom's Buick." Tom pointed to a navy-blue Skylark in the lot.

"I don't want to leave you here without a ride. Better make sure it's hers." Nick pulled into the space next to the car. "I'll wait."

"Why don't you come in with me?" Tom said with an imploring look. "It's some ladies' circle meeting. The place will be crawling with women. I don't want to be the only guy."

Nick could have pointed out that Pastor Schmidt would probably be there, or that there was really nothing to fear from a group of women but he got out of the car and followed Tom into the church.

It didn't take them long to find Mandy. She was in the foyer talking animatedly to a whole gaggle of females. When Nick heard the word *Halloween*, he had to smile. He couldn't wait to tell Taylor.... His smile faded.

"Nick, man. Thanks so much." The boy reached into his back pocket and pulled out a well-worn wallet. "What do I owe you?"

Nick shook his head. "Not a thing."

"But—"

"What are friends for?" That Nick referred to the boy with that term surprised even him. But hadn't the pastor said, in one of those sermons that Nick couldn't seem to get out of his mind, that they were all friends in Christ?

"Thanks so much." Tom pumped his hand vigorously.

"Nick Lanagan." Pastor Schmidt's office door was open, and the minister stuck his head into the hall. "I thought I heard your voice. Do you have a minute?"

Nick forced a smile, hoping the minister didn't want to talk about the wedding that was never going to take place. Today had been hard enough. "Sure."

The minister opened the door wider and ushered Nick inside. "I just got through reviewing the questionnaire I had you and Taylor complete at the last premarital session."

Nick remembered that pop quiz all too well. They'd all thought the evening was almost over when the pastor had surprised them with the survey. Not only did each couple get no chance to discuss the questions, he'd also separated the men and women while they'd filled out the form. Nick had tried his best to anticipate Taylor's answers when he'd written his own. "Did I pass?"

Was it his imagination or did it seem like the minister was hesitating? "Don't tell me I failed?"

"Failed isn't the right word." Pastor Schmidt lifted a coffeepot.

The man was clearly stalling. Unease settled in the pit of Nick's stomach.

"Okay, give me the bad news," Nick said with a little laugh. "You've discovered Taylor and I aren't compatible."

"I wouldn't say that." The minister handed Nick a steaming mug. "At least not just on the basis of a questionnaire."

Even though a dozen words stood poised on the tip of his tongue, Nick took a sip of the coffee and didn't respond. He'd learned the value in the business world of keeping silent until all the cards were on the table.

"There were some points that I did want to discuss with you."

Nick raised a brow.

"Children, for example."

Children? How could they have missed that one? Taylor had made it clear she'd wanted six children, so he'd made sure he'd put down six.

"Are you aware Taylor's not sure that she even wants children? And you put down six."

Nick choked on his coffee.

"I see it is a surprise." The pastor let out a long, audible breath. "The fact that you two haven't discussed it adds to my concern."

Taylor must have thought he'd answer honestly. The minister had stressed that in his instructions. "Above all, be honest," he'd said.

Nick cleared his throat. "We have discussed it, Pastor. What surprised me is that I thought Taylor had agreed to a...big family."

"She can't just agree." The minister leaned forward, his gaze intense. "Taylor needs to really *want* those children, not just do it for you."

At any other time this whole situation would be laughable, her taking his position and his needing to act like he embraced hers.

"I think Taylor has just been concerned that with work and everything else she might not have time for children."

"And what do you say to that?"

Nick resisted the urge to unbutton his suddenly tight collar. "I, uh, tell her that you have to look at what's really important. Your priorities should guide those decisions."

Now it was the minister's turn to raise a brow, and Nick realized he wasn't going to be let off the hook quite so easily. He remembered what Taylor had said, and he made her words his own. "I believe if you put God and family first you can't go wrong. If that means scaling down your work hours, so be it."

"Do you think Taylor would be willing to do that?"

"I do," Nick said. "In fact we've talked about her staying home after we have children."

"She'd be willing to do that?" The minister was

clearly skeptical. "With her career being so important?"

"What is life about if you don't have someone to love?" Nick realized with a start he wasn't just mouthing the words, he believed them. "And this is the electronic age. There are ways to work at home. For both of us."

"I'm glad to hear you say that." The minister flashed a relieved smile. "Anyone can see how much in love the two of you are. I didn't want there to be any insurmountable problems."

"Insurmountable problems?" Nick shook his head and set his cup down. "There's no problem that Taylor and I can't work out. That is, with God's help."

"Nick!" Surprise followed quickly by pleasure flashed through his mother's eyes.

"I probably should have called." He shifted uncomfortably from one foot to the other. In the two years since she'd remarried, he'd never been to her home. But after talking to the minister about the importance of family, he'd decided the time had come to clear the air and mend some fences. "If I'm interrupting…"

"Nonsense." She grabbed his arm and practically yanked him across the threshold. "I'm just puttering around. Charlie is out golfing. Can you believe it? In this heat? I don't know what that man was thinking.''

She chattered all the way into the living room. It was as if she thought he'd disappear if she stopped to take a breath. "Can I get you some iced tea? Or I can brew some coffee?''

"Mother." His hand gripped her arm. "Could we just talk?''

A stricken look crossed her face, and he cursed any and all of his past behavior that had put that look there.

"I need your help," he said softly.

"Is it the company?''

It was understandable she'd think it was work-related. The firm had been his life for the past four years. "No, it's not about work.''

She gestured for him to take a seat, and instead of sitting on the sofa next to him, she took the over-stuffed chair opposite him. Her face, which had been flushed with happiness and animated, was now pale and subdued. "What's the matter, Nick?''

"Were you and Dad happy together?" It wasn't the way he'd wanted to start the conversation, but the question had nagged at him for years.

"Happy?" Clearly caught off guard, she sat back against the plump cushion. "What a strange question.''

"Are you and Charlie happy?''

"Yes, of course.''

"Then why is it so odd for me to ask about you and Dad?"

His mother smoothed an imaginary wrinkle out of her crisp linen slacks. "Your father was a wonderful man with any number of fine qualities."

"Mother." Nick shot her a warning gaze.

She sighed heavily and offered Nick a beseeching look. "I always loved your father, Nick. But I have to admit toward the end, I didn't always like him that much."

"That couldn't have had something to do with the spending, could it?" Old habits died hard, and Nick couldn't stop his cynicism from showing.

Surprisingly, his mother didn't seem to take offense.

"To some extent it did," she said matter-of-factly, a shadow crossing her face. "When we were first married we were happy. But as the business began to grow, he began to spend more time at the office. We grew in different directions. We wanted different things in life. Especially that last year when he felt it was so important to keep up appearances."

Nick's breath caught in his throat. "Appearances?"

"You remember how he was." She shook her head. "Such a private man. When he started staying at home because he didn't have the energy to go to work, he worried about the rumors. To counter the speculation that the business was in trouble, he increased his spending rather than scaling back. He insisted we be seen at all the best parties.''

''All that spending was his idea?'' Nick stared in disbelief.

Sylvia stared back at him. ''Well, of course. You know that. Take buying the Jag, for instance. He'd ordered it before he was diagnosed and he wouldn't hear of pulling the order. 'My dear,' he said, 'what would people think?' I mean, I'm glad that you've gotten your use out of it, but it was hardly a needed purchase. Much less a practical one.'' A trace of bitterness colored her voice. ''He didn't seem to understand that his extravagant spending was putting the entire company at risk.''

She was telling the truth. Nick could see it in her eyes. He cursed his foolishness. All these years he'd blamed her when it had been his father who'd pushed the company to the edge of bankruptcy.

He buried his face in his hands. If he was wrong about this, what else had he been wrong about?

''Nick.'' Soft and concerned, his mother's voice broke through his thoughts. She'd moved from the chair to sit beside him. Her hand rested lightly on his arm. ''Tell me what's wrong.''

He looked into her blue eyes, so like his own, and his heart twisted. What kind of man would have turned away from his own mother because of money? What kind of man would push away the woman he loved because of misplaced pride? What kind of man?

*A fool.* That's what kind of man.

"Mother." Nick reached over and took her hand. "I know I haven't been the kind of son you deserved." He silenced her protest with a raised hand. "But I'm here to tell you that's going to change."

*And that's not the only thing,* he thought. *That's not all that's going to change.*


"He's near the breaking point," Claire said with a satisfied smile. "It's time to go in for the kill."

"In for the kill?" For a second Tony wondered if this was worth the money—until he remembered what Claire was paying him. Yes, the hassle was definitely worth it. Especially if Lanagan was the jerk Claire claimed. "What do you have in mind?"

"Have him find you and Taylor in bed." She leaned forward, and her brown eyes sparkled.

"Not going to happen." He tried to keep the exasperation out of his voice. The woman had a one-track mind. "I've told you what Taylor is like."

Her gaze narrowed, and he wished he hadn't been quite so adamant. Obviously no wasn't a word Claire liked to hear.

"Maybe it's not her," Claire said with a decidedly malicious gleam in her eyes. "Didn't you tell me you were a geek in high school? Maybe you didn't appeal to her.''

"Do I look like a geek to you?" He ripped out the words impatiently.

"Exactly my point," she said. A smile of satisfaction crossed her face. Strange as it seemed, Tony got the impression his irritation pleased her. "Ever hear the saying the past does not determine the future?"

Tony shrugged. "I guess."

"Keep it in mind when you're putting the moves on Taylor. Remember, just because you didn't score before, doesn't mean you're doomed to failure forever." Claire squeezed in next to him. Her breath was warm against his ear. "You can do it. I know you can.''

He turned his face to hers, and she brushed her lips against his. "That's for luck. Now remember, all you have to do is make Nick believe his sweet little Taylor has been unfaithful. If nothing happens just do the next best thing…say you did.''

"Then what?"

"He'll dump Taylor."

A sense of unease coursed through Tony. He frowned. Something wasn't making sense here. "If everything you say about him is true, why would you want him?''

"Because unlike Taylor, I like my guys bad." Claire laughed and ran a long red fingernail up Tony's cheek. "In fact, the badder, the better.''

# Chapter Seventeen

Taylor jerked on the mower cord for what seemed the hundredth time and wondered if it was worth it. She'd thought mowing the yard would help keep her mind off her troubles. But the mower refused to start, and her stress level was rising, along with the temperature outside. A trickle of moisture trailed down her neck.

"What do you think you're doing?" Tony's amused voice sounded from the driveway.

Startled, Taylor glanced up. Her friend stood leaning against his Jeep Cherokee looking cool and perfectly groomed. Feeling even more like a limp dishrag, Taylor blew at a piece of hair that straggled across her forehead. "What does it look like I'm doing? I'm trying to get this machine to start. I need to harvest this yard before the neighbors have me evicted.''

She wiped the sweat from her eyes with the back of her hand and leaned over the mower. She pulled hard on the cord. Once again the engine sputtered. For a second she swore it laughed.

"I'd say it's time for a break." Tony's lips twitched. He crooked one finger and beckoned to her. "Before you kill it or it kills you."

Taylor shot a sideways kick at the mower and walked to the drive.

"I've missed you," he said softly. His gaze traveled over her face and searched her eyes. "Is everything okay?"

"I'm afraid now is not the time to ask." Taylor couldn't help but laugh. "I'm hot and extremely frustrated. Want to come inside for some tea?"

Tony smiled. A confident, lazy smile. "I'd love to."

He followed her into the kitchen, and she could feel his eyes watching her while she filled two crystal tumblers with iced tea and sat them on the table.

She took a seat across the table from him. "Okay, what's up?"

Her directness seemed to take him by surprise. "Does something have to be? Can't a friend just stop by?"

"C'mon, Tony." Taylor had known him too long

to fall for that line. "Something's on your mind. I can tell."

Tony shifted as if his chair had suddenly turned from smooth cherry wood to a seat of nails. "I wanted to talk to you about Nick."

"What about us?" Surely Nick wasn't already telling people they'd broken up? A pain pierced her heart.

"Be honest with me. Aren't you sorry you agreed to marry him?" Tony's dark eyes never left hers for an instant.

Taylor hesitated. There were many things she was sorry for, but agreeing to marry Nick wasn't one of them. And as far as she knew, she was still his fiancée. She cleared her throat and forced a laugh. "Not at all. Why would you even think that?"

Tony's eyes narrowed. "Because from what I've heard, Lanagan seems to be a guy whose only real love is that company of his."

Taylor stiffened. A chill traveled along her spine. "That's ridiculous."

A shadow of hurt flickered across his face. "I'm sorry you think a friend's caring about what happens to you is ridiculous."

He pushed his chair back and started to rise. She leaned forward and grabbed his arm to stop him, her fingers curving in a firm grip.

"Tony, I didn't say you were ridiculous, and I

certainly didn't mean to hurt you." She offered him an apologetic smile. "I just know Nick's not like that."

"He could—"

"Tony, no." Taylor pushed aside her doubts and kept her gaze firm and direct. She thought about Nick's kindness to Miss Dietrich, how he'd helped Tom with his car and the respect he'd always shown her grandparents. "Nick's a great guy. He sometimes comes across as self-absorbed but he'd do anything for those he cares about."

He nodded reluctantly. "If you're sure—"

"I am," she said firmly.

Tony's gaze traveled slowly across her face. "You love him."

"What?"

"You love him," he repeated, amazement blanketing his features.

"Of course I do." She twisted the diamond on her finger. "I'm engaged to the man. I told you from the first that I loved him."

"I know you did." He shook his head. "But I never saw it in your eyes. Until now."

He reached across the table and took her hand. "If he's the right one, then I'm happy for you, Taylor. I'm just not sure that he is."

Taylor stared at this man who had been her friend for so many years. Stared at his dark wavy hair and chiseled features. Stared at the face most women would describe as incredibly handsome. A man so many other women would find easy to love. A man who would forever only be her friend.

"You'll always be special to me."

"And you to me." Abruptly he shoved back his chair and rose to his feet, his smile forced. "I need to get going."

The phone on the counter rang, and Taylor jumped. Before she could stop him Tony leaned over and picked up the receiver. "Hello."

His expression stilled and grew serious. He let out a long audible breath. "She's right here."

Taylor leaned forward, a sense of dread coursing through her veins. "Is it Nick?"

"No." He held the phone out to her, and compassion darkened his eyes. "It's about your grandfather."

# Chapter Eighteen

"Where is he?" Taylor's gaze swept the waiting room. There wasn't even a nurse in sight. Only Nick.

"Back there." Nick scrambled to his feet. He gestured to a closed set of double doors. "The doctor is with him now."

Taylor hated hospitals, all stark and white. The medicinal smell irritated her nose, and the overhead paging of every Code Blue sent fear racing up her spine.

"What room is he in?" Taylor headed for the doors without waiting for an answer. She would have been halfway down the hall if Nick hadn't grabbed her arm.

"Taylor, wait."

"Let me go," she said through gritted teeth.

"Listen to me—"

"Nick, not now." She tried to jerk away, but his grip was too strong. "We can talk later. Right now I want to see my grandfather."

"That's what I'm trying to tell you." His voice was firm. "Only one person can be with him right now, and your grandmother just went back."

Taylor stared, unblinking. All she'd wanted was to see her grandfather one more time and tell him how much she loved him. Just in case he... She shoved the unbearable thought aside and refused to let the tears pressing against her lids fall. He *was* going to make it. She wasn't going to let herself believe otherwise.

"Why don't we sit down?" Nick's voice was gentle and low.

Not trusting herself to speak, Taylor gave a jerky nod and let him lead her over to a smooth green vinyl couch that hugged the waiting room wall. Nick took a seat next to her.

It wasn't until she sat down that she realized how shaky her knees had become. It was a wonder she'd been able to stand at all. She took a deep breath and clenched her hands in her lap. "Tell me what happened."

"He started having chest pains," Nick said in a matter-of-fact, I-don't-want-to-alarm-you voice. "Your grandmother called nine-one-one. She said she tried to reach you at home but no one answered.''

*That stupid mower.*

''She got me on my cellular, and I came right over. She thought you might be with me,'' he added.

Of course her grandmother would have thought that. Nana was the eternal optimist. Even now she probably believed everything would turn out okay.

''Your grandfather will be fine.''

''You don't know that.''

''No, but I've certainly bent God's ear since I've been here,'' Nick said. ''I'm hoping that He'll make Bill well just to shut me up.''

God would be shutting her up, too. Taylor hadn't stopped praying since she got the news. She'd hoped when she'd reached the hospital that her prayers would have been answered. A band tightened around her chest.

''He could be dying in there and I wouldn't even know.'' To her surprise Taylor spoke her fears aloud. She blinked back another round of tears and furiously dug deep in her purse. By the time her fingers closed around the tissue, a few tears streaked her cheeks.

''If they don't come out in five minutes, I'll go back and check,'' Nick said.

''If someone's not here in *two* minutes, *I'll* go check.''

"You're one determined woman." A smile tugged at Nick's lips. She could hear the admiration in his voice. "Taylor?"

She glanced briefly at her watch and then at the closed doors. Ninety seconds left. "Yes?"

His gaze locked with hers, and his blue eyes shimmered in the fluorescent glare. "I'm sorry about this morning."

"It doesn't matter." Again her gaze strayed to the end of the hall.

"I should have told you about the job the minute I found out," he said. "I'm not going to lie to you anymore."

The pain of his betrayal returned. She steeled herself against the ache in her heart. "Nick, we can talk about this some other time?"

"Why not now?"

She drew a deep steadying breath. "Because right now I'm worried about my grandfather and—"

The strident ring of his cell phone stopped her words. She glanced at her watch. Thirty seconds.

"Lanagan." The word was clipped, and she idly wondered if he was irritated with her or if there were problems at work. Either way she didn't care. He raked his fingers through his hair, and his gaze shifted momentarily to her. "Now? Isn't there another time Henry— Erik, you'll have to reschedule.

Of course I understand the risk. Anytime tomorrow would be fine.''

"You can go, Nick. I'm sure you must have a lot of work to do." Taylor rose to her feet. "I'm going to check on Grandpa Bill."

"I'm not going anywhere." He closed the cell phone with a firm snap and stood. "And *we're* going to check on Bill."

"But your phone—"

"Stop." His fingers against her lips stopped the words. "Family is more important than work any day."

In the back of her mind she noted the change in Nick's priorities, but she didn't have time to figure out what it meant. All she knew was having Nick share her burden of worry somehow made the load easier to bear.

"Thanks," she said simply.

"Ms. Rollins, I'm not sure if you remember me...."

Taylor's head jerked in the direction of the unexpected voice. She automatically extended her hand. "Dr. Pierce. Of course I remember you."

The middle-aged doctor looked much the same as he had a year ago, although a few strands of gray laced his black hair. With the white lab coat and a stethoscope looped casually around his neck, he was the picture of competence.

But she knew all too well how looks could deceive. The well-respected cardiologist had been on call the night of her father's accident. But he and the other physicians hadn't been able to save her father. Now Grandpa Bill's life was in his hands. A cold chill rippled through her body.

Nick's arm slipped around her waist and rested lightly against her side in a gesture of silent support.

"How is he?" She forced the words past her lips.

Dr. Pierce hesitated, much as he'd done when he'd given her news of her father's death. Her body went numb. Dear God, had she lost Grandpa Bill, too?

"He's stable. However, I don't want to minimize the potential seriousness of his condition."

Her heart pounded in her ears, and she took a deep breath, willing herself to stay calm.

The doctor's hazel eyes met Taylor's gaze. "His heart is in an irregular rhythm. We could wait and see if we could treat it with medication, but with the angina, it's best to treat it immediately. My associate is doing the procedure now."

"Procedure?" Taylor couldn't keep the tremor from her voice.

"Cardioversion," Dr. Pierce said. "Shock the heart back into normal sinus rhythm."

"It sounds dangerous."

"It can be, but—" a faint smile graced the doctor's face "—your grandfather's remarkably healthy otherwise. We've done a lot of these procedures with good success.''

Nick squeezed her hand reassuringly.

''I'll keep you informed,'' Dr. Pierce said. ''I want to assure you we're doing everything we can.''

''Thanks, Dr. Pierce.'' Taylor swallowed hard against the lump in her throat. ''He and my grandmother are all I have, and I love them both dearly.''

''I understand.'' The doctor nodded before he left, but stopped short of giving her the reassurance she sought.

''What you told the doctor wasn't entirely accurate.'' Nick's voice sounded strained against her ear.

Taylor turned. He stood so close his breath was warm against her cheek. She lifted her gaze.

''You also have me,'' he said.

''For now,'' she said. *But for how long?*

Tony took a sip of coffee, keeping his gaze focused on the door to the restaurant.

Claire was late, as usual. He'd grown tired of waiting in the lobby so he'd taken a table by the window. Getting a seat in the normally busy eatery hadn't been a problem at this time of day. The large room was empty except for a group of businessmen at a large round table to the back.

Tony's gaze dropped to the airline ticket lying

on the table. After leaving Taylor, he'd stopped at the local travel agency and booked his flight. Ten tomorrow he'd be on that big bird winging its way from Denver to D.C. He couldn't wait.

"I thought I said to wait in the lobby." Although Claire's words were censuring, she brushed her lips across his cheek before taking a seat opposite him.

"You also said we'd meet at three," he said, taking another sip of coffee.

"You're such a clock-watcher." She wrinkled her nose and picked up a menu. She didn't apologize for being a half-hour late, but then he never expected she would. That wasn't Claire Waters.

He gestured to the waiter.

"What can I get you?" The server couldn't have been more than twenty, tanned with blond streaked hair, looking like he'd just stepped off a ski slope.

Claire preened under the man's openly admiring gaze. Tony had to admit she looked especially beautiful today. She'd pulled her dark hair from her face in one of the new trendy styles, and her makeup made her brown eyes appear even larger.

"I'll have a glass of strawberry apricot iced tea," she said.

The young man smiled, showing a mouthful of straight white teeth. "Will that be all?"

"For now," Claire said, looking up at him through thickly mascaraed lashes.

Tony resisted the overwhelming urge to gag.

Her gaze followed the waiter until he disappeared into the kitchen.

"You'd be robbing the cradle with that one," Tony pointed out.

"He's cute." Her smile was openly appreciative. "Did you notice?"

"I'll make sure to look when he comes back."

Her eyes narrowed, and he knew she'd finally picked up on the coolness in his tone. Her hand reached over and blanketed his. "Don't be jealous."

"Jealous?" Tony snorted. "As if."

A flash of hurt skittered across her face, and she jerked her hand back.

"Claire, I'm sorry."

"Let's get down to business." Her gaze hardened. "Did you succeed in your mission?"

Tony cleared his throat and shifted his gaze to the waiter.

Openly curious, the young man took his time lifting a tumbler filled with tea and chipped ice off a round tray before setting it on the linen tablecloth in front of Claire.

"That'll be all for now," Tony said, not giving the waiter—or Claire—a chance to speak.

Tony waited until the young man was out of sight before he spoke. He didn't bother to hide his annoyance. "And what if I did succeed? Do you plan to broadcast it to the world?"

"You did it!" Joy flashed across Claire's face.

Tony relished the knowledge her happiness would be short-lived.

"Actually I didn't even try." He sat his cup down, lifted his gaze and waited for the explosion.

She glared at him. "What kind of game are you playing?"

Instead of a shriek, her voice was low and controlled. His estimation of her inched up a notch.

"No game." For the first time since he'd come to Cedar Ridge, Tony felt at peace with himself. "Taylor's my friend. She's in love with Nick. End of story."

Claire leaned across the table, her dark eyes spitting fire. "No, it's not the end. I've paid you a lot of money—"

"I'll pay you back." He'd made that decision after leaving Taylor's house.

"With what?" She sneered. "Your good looks?"

He deserved the jab. From the moment they'd met he'd shown her only his shallow, superficial side. He hadn't always been that way. Seeing Taylor again had brought back old memories, old dreams.

For the first time since he'd been a teen he found himself looking toward the future. Even considering again one particular dream he'd cast aside long ago.

It was almost as if he'd been given a second chance. He was back on track once again.

*Thank you, God.*

He smiled at Claire, praying she would one day find the sense of peace he'd rediscovered.

No, nothing was going to stop him now.

Unless, he mused, staring at Claire's thunderous expression, she killed him first.


Taylor let the hospital room door close silently behind her.

"He wants to talk to you." Utterly drained, she brushed a strand of hair from her face.

Thankfully, Grandpa Bill looked much better than she'd expected. But the day's strain had caught up with her.

Concern blanketed Nick's face. "Are you okay?"

"I'm fine." Taylor forced a smile. She hadn't been sure he'd still be here when she came out. She'd asked him to come in with her, but he'd said he thought they needed some time alone as a family. "Would you mind staying with my grandfather for a few minutes? He wants to see you," she added.

"I'm sure your grandmother—"

"Is going to go to the cafeteria," Taylor said, his hesitation taking her by surprise. If she didn't know better she'd think he didn't want to face the man.

But that didn't make sense. Over the past months, Nick and her grandfather had become fast friends.

Nick shifted uneasily from one foot to the other.

"Please, Nick." She rested her hand lightly on his arm. "Even if you won't do it for me, Nana needs to get some food in her stomach, but she won't leave him alone."

He stared for a moment, then nodded. "Sure. I'll stay with him."

"Thank you." Her voice shook slightly. She clamped her lips together. The emotional upheaval of the past twenty-four hours threatened to derail her carefully held composure.

"Hey." Nick tipped up her chin with one finger. "Don't go getting all weepy on me."

"I'm not," she retorted, the moisture behind her lids evaporating in a spark of anger. She'd never been a woman who cried at the drop of a hat, and he'd been around her long enough to know that. "I have…"

If the twinkle in his eyes wasn't enough, the twitch of his lips said it all.

She chuckled. "What am I going to do with you?"

His voice dropped, and a strange look filled his eyes. "I don't know. Maybe keep me around a while longer? Maybe—"

"Nana." Taylor cleared her throat and smiled at her grandmother over Nick's shoulder. "Nick has agreed to stay with Grandpa while we grab a bite to eat.''

Her grandmother shook her head. "I'm really not hungry."

"Nana, you haven't eaten all day." Taylor slipped her arm around her grandmother's shoulders. "And even if you're not hungry, I'm starved."

"Kaye, go ahead and keep Taylor company. It'll give me a chance to talk to Bill. There's something I want to discuss with him." Nick sounded so sincere that even Taylor was impressed.

"If you're positive you can spare the time?" Nana hesitated. "I'm sure you've got lots of work to do."

"Nothing that can't wait." Nick voice was firm and broached no argument.

Still Nana waffled. "What if they need to reach me? Sometimes you can't hear or understand those overhead pages."

Taylor glanced at Nick and lifted her shoulders in a silent plea for help. She could understand Nana's reluctance, but her grandmother had to eat.

Nick reached into the pocket of his suit jacket and pulled out his cellular phone. "Take this with you." He waved aside Nana's protests. "With all that monitoring equipment, I can't take it in the room anyway."

Taylor took the phone from his hand. "Thank you."

He smiled. "You ladies take your time. Bill and I will be just fine."

"Thank you, Nick." To Taylor's surprise Nana reached up and brushed a kiss across his cheek.

But when Nick enveloped her grandmother in a hug and whispered, "It will all be okay," Taylor could only stare.

"C'mon, honey." Nana stepped out of Nick's arms and headed for the elevator. "A bowl of soup might be a good idea, after all."

They'd barely made their way through the long cafeteria line and gotten settled in at a table when Nick's phone rang.

Her grandmother stopped cutting her grilled cheese sandwich into fourths. The color drained from her face. She and Taylor exchanged a wordless look of worry.

Taylor flipped open the phone. "Hello."

The cafeteria was in the lower level of the hospital. That fact, coupled with the noise from the supper crowd, made hearing difficult. She pressed one hand against her other ear. "Hello?"

"Nick, it's Erik. We've got a bad connection. I can barely hear you."

"It's for Nick." She mouthed the words to her grandmother, and Nana sighed with relief and turned her attention to her sandwich.

"Nick, can you hear me?" Although filled with static, Erik's words were clearly audible.

"Yes, but—"

"Okay, you listen. I'll talk," Erik interrupted, and Taylor realized if he couldn't tell she wasn't Nick, he probably couldn't hear her well enough to understand her explanation.

"I was able to reschedule that meeting with Henry. You owe me big for this one, buddy. The old barracuda wanted to know what was so important that you wouldn't take time to sign the papers. Asked if you really wanted to merge. Of course, I improvised. Used an idea from a story I'd read in the tabloids and told him you'd been kidnapped by space aliens. I don't think he was fully convinced but at least he laughed. So, two p.m. tomorrow, no excuses. Ciao."

Taylor ended the call in a daze. If she'd understood what Erik had said, Nick had given up a chance to finalize the merger to be here with her and her grandparents. She knew what that deal meant to him. This wasn't making any sense.

"Who was it?" Nana took a bite of sandwich, her look openly curious.

"Nick's lawyer." Taylor frowned. "Apparently Nick canceled an important meeting this afternoon. Why would he have done that?"

"Why, my dear, I should think that would be perfectly obvious." Nana laughed for the first time today, a silver tinkle of a laugh. "The man is in love."

Nana handed Nick the phone and after thanking him profusely went immediately to her husband. Taylor and Nick slipped out of the room unnoticed.

"Thanks for staying with him."

Nick shrugged. "It was nothing."

Taylor took a deep breath and clasped her hands together. "We need to talk."

He gazed into her eyes. Could he hear her heart beating?

"Yes, we do," he said softly. "But not here."

"The cafeteria's out. You can't hear yourself think down there," she said, half to herself. "How about the park? It's just across the street."

"Fine with me." He turned toward the elevator, but she stopped him with a hand on his arm.

"Wait a minute." Taylor stuck her head inside her grandfather's room. "Nick and I are going to take a little walk. Maybe go over to the park and get some fresh air. Will you two be okay?"

Bill smiled at his wife and laid his hand over hers. "We've managed for almost fifty years. I think we can handle a half hour or so."

Taylor smiled and pulled the door shut.

Even though the day was bright and sunny, the park that bordered the hospital grounds was deserted. Taylor spotted a weathered picnic table under a huge elm and took a seat across from Nick.

"Erik called for you." It was an odd way to start a conversation, but Erik's words were foremost on her mind.

"He did?" Nick raised a brow. "What did he have to say?"

"We had a bad connection," Taylor said. "He thought I was you."

"Must have been a really bad connection." Nick smiled. "Erik doesn't usually have any trouble distinguishing men from women."

The dimple in his cheek flashed, and her heart turned over.

"He wanted to let you know the meeting to sign the merger papers was rescheduled for two p.m. tomorrow."

"Good." Nick nodded in satisfaction.

"Why didn't you sign them today?"

"I was busy."

"Busy with us?" She knew more than most what this merger meant and how temperamental Henry could be. "You could have blown the deal by waiting."

"You needed me."

"You should have told me," Taylor persisted. "I would have been okay by myself."

Nick gave a deep, resigned sigh. "The point is I

don't want you to have to be alone. I want to be there for you.''

"That's very sweet." She'd misunderstood his intentions once. She wasn't going to make that mistake again. "But our contract is almost up. Once those papers are signed, we're done.''

"This whole fake engagement thing was a stupid idea.''

Her heart sank. "It was?"

"I don't like being engaged," he added.

"You don't?" Granted it had been awkward at first, but lately it hadn't been a chore, not at all.

"No, I don't." He reached across the table and took her hand.

Taylor tried to force a smile but couldn't quite manage it. "I'm sure you'll change your mind when you find a woman you really want to marry.''

"I've already found her.''

"You have?" For a second she could only stare, stunned. Then something snapped. How could she have ever thought there was a possibility he loved her? "Who is it? No, don't tell me. I don't want to know. What an idiot I've been." Taylor jerked to her feet, feeling like the worst kind of fool.

"No, wait." He scrambled up from the table and stepped in front of her, blocking her exit. "I'm saying this all wrong.''

"You don't need to say more." Taylor blinked away the tears. "You've already said enough.''

"I don't think I have," he said forcefully. "Have I said it's *you* I want to marry? Have I said it's *you* I love?"

She shook her head slowly, not trusting herself to speak.

"See, I didn't say it all." His hand gently brushed her hair over her shoulder. "I love you, Taylor. It's taken me longer than it should have, but I finally realize what's important in life."

"What about the company?"

"It matters to me. I can't say that it doesn't. But I was wrong to put it first in my life. You were right. God and family deserve top billing."

"Are you sure?"

"I'm positive." His hand cupped her face. "Will you marry me, Taylor? I'm asking for real this time."

She longed to shout her answer to the treetops, but one last piece of unfinished business held her back. "Nick, remember when you said no more lies?"

"I'm not lying—"

She closed his lips with her fingers. "You've been honest with me. Now I need to be honest with you."

Praying for strength, Taylor took a deep breath and told him what she'd kept to herself for so long. She told him the story of her father's gambling debts and her attempt to protect his reputation.

Somewhere in the middle of the story, his hand slipped down her arm, and he laced his fingers through hers. When she finished, he wiped a few stray tears from her cheeks with his fingers.

"You must have felt so alone." His arms wrapped around her, and his voice was muffled against her hair. "I wish I'd known sooner."

Her heart warmed. Instead of focusing on what her father had done, his whole concern was on her feelings.

"I'm just glad you're here now." She lifted her head, and her eyes met his.

"Me, too." His gaze was warm against her face. "You never did answer my question."

"Maybe I need a little reminder."

"Of the question?"

She laughed. "No, of how much you love me."

A thrill of anticipation shot through her as he lowered his head.

"Will this do?" he murmured against her lips.

"For now," she said returning his kiss. Oh, yes, for now it would do just fine.

The nurse handed Bill the last of the paperwork.

Standing by the window, Nana barely noticed. Her gaze was riveted outdoors, on something more fascinating than any insurance forms.

"You're doing great. Your heart has stayed in normal sinus rhythm, and," the nurse added, "once we get your meds up from the pharmacy, you'll be ready for discharge.''

"Hear that, Kaye?" Bill rubbed his hands together. "Sounds like everything's going to be just fine."

Nana glanced briefly at her husband before her gaze returned to the window overlooking the park. A smile of satisfaction lifted her lips. Today had been filled with blessings.

*Thank You, God.*

"Kaye?"

She turned to her husband. "What did you say, sweetheart?"

"I said everything has worked out just fine."

"Yes," Nana said. "Yes, it has."

# *Chapter Nineteen*

"**I** can't believe they knew all along about my father's debts." Taylor's gaze followed her grandparents on the dance floor.

"I'm sure your father would have eventually told you, too," Nick said. "But if you hadn't been so desperate for money, you wouldn't have agreed to be my fiancée, and we wouldn't be here now."

"I think God would have found a way to get us together," Taylor said, softly brushing her fingers against his cheek.

The sound of five hundred pieces of silver clinking against crystal goblets filled the ballroom of the Heritage Hotel.

Nick turned to his new bride and smiled. "Shall we?"

"It *is* tradition," Taylor said with mock resignation, even as her lips curved in a smile.

Nick lifted his napkin off his lap and dropped it to the linen-clad table. He pushed back his chair and stood, reaching for her hand.

Her fingers were warm against his skin, and a faint whiff of perfume stirred his senses. She turned and raised her arms so that her hands rested lightly on his shoulders. Her face tilted upward, waiting for his kiss.

Never had she looked more beautiful. He thanked God once again for the love and trust reflected in her gaze. Out of the corner of his eye he caught a glimpse of his mother and stepfather smiling proudly.

Yes, he had a lot to be thankful for.

"Are you going to kiss her or just stand there looking like a love-struck fool?" Henry's voice boomed from a nearby table.

Nick's smile widened, and he lowered his lips to his new bride, forcing himself to keep the kiss light and brief. There'd be time for more later. Much more.

The guests clapped. Nick chuckled. Taylor's cheeks turned pink. They sat down, and Nick rested his arm around the back of Taylor's chair, glad to be out of the spotlight. Unfortunately it didn't last long.

He stifled a groan as Erik pushed back his chair and stood, a mischievous glint in his eye.

"As the best man, I believe a toast is indicated." Erik lifted his glass of champagne, his gaze focused on Taylor and Nick. "I've known Nick for a long time, and he's made some smart moves in the past—hiring me as his attorney comes immediately to mind—but hanging on to Taylor wasn't just a smart move, it was a brilliant one. Seeing how happy they are almost makes me want to get married. Almost. But truly, Nick, Taylor, may you have a long and happy life together. Go forth and multiply."

Abruptly Erik sat down amidst laughter and a round of applause.

"Thank you, Erik." Nick rose, his smile widening. "That part about multiplying sounds especially intriguing."

Laughter erupted once again, but died down when Nick turned to the audience of friends and family, his face serious. "I'd like to take this opportunity to do a toast. I've said it before but never have I meant it more than I do at this minute." He raised his goblet, and his voice rang strong and firm in the silence. "To the woman who made me realize that I could have all the riches in the world but be poor without her by my side. To my lovely Taylor, my best friend, my love, and now, my wife. I am truly blessed."

By the time he finished, Taylor's eyes glistened with tears. Nana dabbed at her eyes with the tip of a napkin, and Grandpa Bill cleared his throat. Even Nick had a lump in his throat, thinking how far they'd come.

He sat down and impulsively brushed a kiss across Taylor's lips. "I love you, Mrs. Lanagan."

Her fingers brushed his cheek. "I love you, too, Mr. Lanagan."

"Break it up, you two." Grandpa Bill leaned across the table. "There's plenty of time for that later."

"We're just getting warmed up," Nick said with a grin. "Erik did tell us to be fruitful and multiply."

"For once, a member of this family that listens to me." Erik laughed. "I threw that in because Bill over here was telling me you and Taylor want a big family. I couldn't believe it." His friend eyed him with a calculating expression. "You really want six kids?"

Nick's gaze slid across the crowded room. Past the little ring bearer in his tux dancing with the flower girl, past the children at the various tables nestled between their parents. He thought of what Taylor had taught him, about what is really important in life.

He leaned over and wrapped Taylor's hand in his before turning to Erik with a smile he didn't try to hide. "Hey, call me crazy. But I really do."

\* \* \* \* \*

Dear Reader,

In *The Marrying Kind,* Nick Lanagan has a lesson
to learn. Somewhere along the way he lost touch with
what's really important in life. He's put his career first,
and although his professional life is flourishing, his
personal life is floundering.

Taylor helps him to rethink his priorities and to
realize that he's never going to be able to achieve true
happiness until he embraces one simple truth: that God
and family come first. It's a lesson we should all take to
heart.

I hope you enjoy the book!

Warmly,

Cynthia Rutledge

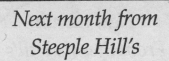